HIS FRACTURED BUTTERFLY

DEANN F. JONES

Contents

Author's Note
Trigger Warnings

Dear Reader,

Thank you for picking up *His Fractured Butterfly*. I want to take a moment to address the themes and content within this book that some readers may find distressing. This story delves into the complexities of human experience, including moments of deep pain and struggle. As a result, it contains the following triggers:

- Violence

- Sexual Content

- Sexual Assault

- Emotional Abuse

- Mental Illness

- Substance Abuse

- Death

- Domestic Violence

I recognize these topics can be deeply upsetting, and I encourage you to prioritize your well-being as you read. If at any point you find the content overwhelming, please feel free to take a break or step away from the book.

My intention in exploring these difficult themes is to shed light on the resilience of the human spirit and the power of healing. However, I understand that each reader's experience is unique, and I want to ensure that you feel safe and supported as you engage with this story.

Thank you for your understanding and for allowing me to share this narrative with you.

With care,

DeAnn F. Jones

Chapter One

Goodbye

(2002)

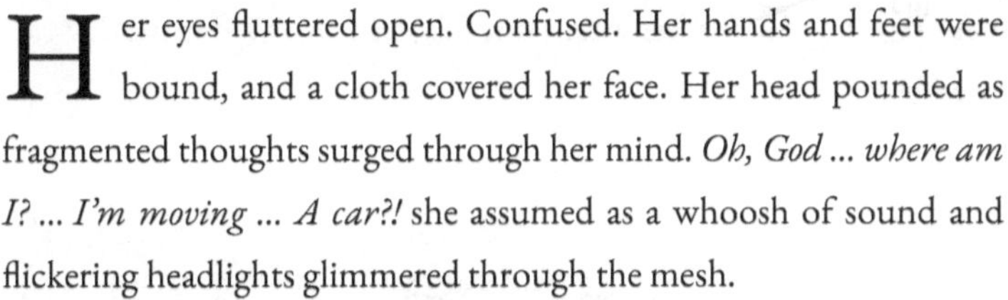

Her eyes fluttered open. Confused. Her hands and feet were bound, and a cloth covered her face. Her head pounded as fragmented thoughts surged through her mind. *Oh, God ... where am I? ... I'm moving ... A car?!* she assumed as a whoosh of sound and flickering headlights glimmered through the mesh.

A wave of panic gripped her as the lingering haze from whatever they knocked her out with dissipated. She gasped for breath as the stark awareness of her dire situation took hold.

Her screams, stifled by the tape holding her mouth shut, muted her desperate pleas. Her wriggling became an involuntary signal to her captors that consciousness had now returned.

"There is no use fighting," a deep, gruff voice with a thick Romanian accent echoed as she struggled from somewhere in front of her.

"We're taking you home, little lady, back to the States," another male voice crooned, but this accent was different, British, cockney maybe? He was closer, beside her; she could feel him lean over her as she struggled. His hand stroked the outside of the cloth covering her face as he spoke.

Daria thrashed against her restraints. "Let me go, you bastards!" she shouted, her voice still muffled and strained with desperation.

"Oh, she's a feisty little thing, this one," the Brit remarked, his tone laced with amusement

She kicked the back of the seat in front of her, causing the driver to jerk the steering wheel.

"Calm yourself. We do not want to hurt you. Your benefactors would be very upset if you were harmed," he spoke to her directly, then to the Brit, "Put her to sleep again before we get to the airport."

"Aye, Gov."

A rustling caught her attention, followed by the sharp prick of a needle ...

Awake again, her head mercifully free from the pounding this time. She found herself on a cold and grimy wood floor. The shroud that had been covering her head and the tape that sealed her mouth, now removed, granted her a welcome reprieve, allowing her to breathe more easily, but her hands and feet were still bound.

Darkness blanketed the room, with only faint glimmers of pale blue light filtering through the slats of wood that appeared to barely support the roof above. The cool, damp morning air chilled her, carrying the scent of earth with a hint of mold that tickled her nose.

She sat still, in and out of consciousness, trying to regain her faculties as the sunrise crept through the ripped curtains of a broken window across from her. A piece of the remaining glass refracted a ray of light, blinding her for a second as another cool breeze blew through, fully waking her and allowing the morning light to flood the room.

It revealed a young man sitting on the floor, his legs crossed in front of him, and his back propped against the wall, dozing beneath the window. He wasn't restrained, and a surge of panic rose in her throat as she eyed him.

His dusty blonde hair curled up from under a baseball cap turned backward on his head. He appeared to be around six feet tall and slender. She couldn't help but acknowledge his rugged appearance with fair, sun-kissed skin, sharp features, and at least a two-day growth on his chin. Not at all how she pictured her captors.

Daria tried to wiggle out of her bindings, waking him. He opened one blue eye and peeked up at her.

"You're awake," he croaked and stretched. "You been out a long time."

She looked at him through squinted eyes and spat, "Why am I here?" He may not have been one of her captors, but he wasn't tied when she woke, so odds were, he wasn't there to help her either.

He stood and walked over to her. "I was told to be careful … you might be difficult when you wake up. That's why I left you tied." he paused and knelt in front of her. "Are you gonna be … difficult?" He cocked his head.

"Why. Am. I. Here?" More determined this time.

"Well, I don't know why yer here, little girl, but I'm supposed ta be meetin' my new bride. And I don't suppose that'd be you. Yer just a young'n ain't cha," he joked and cocked his head back to look down his nose at her. "How old are ya, anyway?"

"Where are we?" she cried, ignoring his query.

"Calm down, girl! Now, I ain't supposed to tell you that right now. But I will unbind you if you stay calm."

Daria held her hands out for him to release her bindings. "Just hold on now," he warned, "you ain't agreed to be calm yet."

She took a deep breath and sighed. "I'll be calm," she said finally through gritted teeth as she pushed her hands even closer to him.

"Okay. Okay. Hold yer britches."

He pulled a pocketknife from his back pocket, causing her to flinch as he unfolded it. He worked to cut her hands free first, then looked her over as he sawed at the tape still binding her feet. She sat stone still, her eyes fixed on him, watching his every move.

"You sure are a pretty little thing; I hope my bride is as handsome a woman as you are, young'n."

"You can't be that much older than me, so stop calling me young'n."

"Ha, I'll have you know I'm a man of twenty-four years," he said proudly. "Why you ain't much older than, what? Thirteen, fourteen?"

"I'm eighteen, for your information," she said, squinting a glare at him.

"I don't believe that fer a minute."

"Well, it's true. Everyone says I look like a kid without makeup, but—" She stopped herself, realizing she shouldn't reveal too much. Then exasperation set in, and she blurted, "And anyway, my boyfriend is the same age as you. When he finds me, you're gonna be in deep shit!"

He finished cutting the binds on her feet as she spoke, then held his hands up in surrender. "Whoa, whoa now, I ain't done nothin' to you. Those men just dropped you off and said, 'Take good care of her'."

"Who were they?!"

"Never seen 'em before. They talked funny, though."

"Really? So do you," she said, cocking her head sarcastically, noting his deep southern drawl.

She spoke up, feeling unafraid and somewhat relieved that this young man was not involved in her kidnapping. "I don't understand. Why are you even out here? Why would you choose this place to meet your bride?"

"The sheriff dropped me off and told me to wait here for him. Then you showed up." He sniffed. "I made a deal with this judge. He said if I was to marry this old guy's niece and stay out of trouble, they wouldn't throw me back in the hoosegow."

"You mean jail?"

"Yeah, and I ain't going back there. He said I'd be taken care of. Not want for nothin' ... sounded like a good deal to me, so I took it."

The main door opened, catching their attention; it was the sheriff. Both looked up at him. "Good, you've met," he said. "C'mere boy." The young man stood and walked over to him.

The sheriff took his ten-gallon hat off and tucked it up under his arm, then handed the young man some papers.

"Here's yer marriage license and yer new state IDs." The sheriff held a set of keys in the air and dropped them into the young man's other hand. "Yer address is on yer ID, and there's a truck outside I'm supposed to leave with you. You got any questions?"

Daria was about to jump up and beg for the sheriff's help as the young man looked at the papers, then back at him and asked, "So, where's this bride I'm supposed to be meetin'?"

The sheriff pointed at Daria and said, "Yer lookin' at her."

Both speaking simultaneously, "What?!"

The young man protested, "I can't marry her; she's just a child!"

"You're already married, and she's of consenting age. We checked. Besides, I'd say you got the better end of this deal, boy!" The sheriff slapped him on the shoulder as he looked over at Daria, giving her a wink and a nod, then said, "Congratulations, ma'am." He put his hat back on, turned, and walked out, chuckling.

Still on the floor, Daria sat, stunned. *What the hell just happened?* She thought. *This has to be a mistake. No way am I married to that country bumpkin. I already have a boyfriend, he'll be looking for me, and so will my family. Jesus, this can't be hap—*

"Welp, I guess we better get this here honeymoon started," the young man said as he tossed the keys and caught them effortlessly in one hand. He walked towards the door, but as he passed the doorjamb, he noticed she hadn't moved. He stopped, leaned back in, and said, "Well, come on, little woman, we ain't got all day!"

Daria stood, brushed herself off, then hesitated before trailing him to the door. She called out to him, "Hey, uh ... I don't even know your name!"

He looked down at his ID and held it up for inspection. "Levi, according to this here, ID. My name is Levi Stratton," he said with a smile before heading towards the truck.

"And mine would be?"

He rifled through the papers. "Your Diary, no, Diar—"

"Daria?" she corrected him.

"Yeah, Daria. That's right, Daria Stratton."

"Huh?" she thought. *"Why would they change his entire name and not mine? Maybe because he's a felon, Daria—duh! I doubt anyone is looking for any Darias here anyway, wherever here is. Oh hey, maybe he can—"*

"Hey, Levi, could you drop me off at the nearest phone?"

"Oh, no, MA'AM! No, no, no, see, I made a deal with that there judge, and I aim to keep my word! Besides, I think I'm takin' a likin' to ya! Come on now, get a move on!"

Once she stepped foot onto the porch, an expansive oak and hickory forest greeted her, its thick canopy casting long shadows that stretched toward the sky, almost eclipsing the rising sun.

The onset of fall had transformed the woodlands into a breathtaking tapestry of brownish-orange and golden leaves. With each passing breeze, leaves trickled down like rain. Evidently, they had spent the night in a weathered turn-of-the-century homesteaders' cabin, probably in a national park somewhere.

She put her hands on her hips and surveyed her surroundings, appreciating the beauty and trying to focus on the task at hand—escape. As a crisp breeze hit her bare arms, she warmed herself by rubbing them up and down. She looked back towards the truck and Levi, noting the one dirt road that led in and out.

Well, shit. Daria stood glaring at her new husband in protest. She watched Levi get into the driver's seat, put the keys in the ignition, and turn the engine over. She saw his distraction as her chance to flee. *If I can get away from him and hide, I can walk out later.* She took off sprinting towards the rear of the cabin, counting on its structure to shield her from his line of sight. The pounding of her footsteps echoed through the air as she sought refuge, hoping to vanish from his immediate view.

Levi's gaze snapped up from the dashboard, realizing she had disappeared. "Dammit, girl!" He leaped out, running toward the cabin. He stopped when he couldn't see her, then, hearing the snapping of twigs, he headed in that direction.

Daria, driven by a desperate need to put distance between herself and Levi, darted aimlessly through the woods. Her path led her downhill, getting steeper the further she ran. She slipped on the damp leaves that covered the forest floor, her footing precarious. She realized Levi was getting closer, hearing the heavy tromping of boots behind her. When she turned to look, she tripped, tumbling over the edge of a low rock cliff, and landed with a loud 'Oomph.'

She assessed her injuries as she sat at the bottom, one leg twisted behind her. Only noticing a few scratches, she attempted to stand. *OW! Now what!* Her leg collapsed out from under her, and tears pricked her eyes as she fell to the ground in defeat. Her knee pulsated as pain radiated through her entire leg.

In a millisecond, her brain attempted to process the situation and determine a response. Hurt, frustrated, scared, and just plain angry—complex emotions flooded her mind, leaving her without a rational course of action. Ultimately, she could only express her overwhelming feelings with a single word. "FUUUCK!"

Levi came around the corner of the rock cliff and stood, hands on his knees, catching his breath. He waited to see if she'd try to escape again, but then he realized she was hurt. "I guess we're doing this the hard way," he said. "That's a'right. I like the hard way." He smiled as he headed toward her.

She pointed at him, seeing his wicked smile, and said, "You can't hurt me. They told you to take care of me, remember?"

"Oh, I'm gonna take care of you a'right. Real, good care of ya!" He walked up to her, leaned over, grabbed both of her arms and, in one fell swoop, pulled her over his shoulder.

His strength shocked her. "Put me down!"

"You can't walk."

"Put me down! Put me down!" She kicked with her one good leg.

"Hush, woman! You'll scare the bears!" She stopped yelling, rested her hands on his back to support herself, and turned to look at him over her shoulder.

"Bears? There's bears?"

"I said HUSH!" He popped her on her butt, and she let out a squelched yelp, then scanned the area, looking for any signs of wildlife. Once he settled her in the truck's passenger seat, they set off. Daria sat in silence, pouting, and stubbornly refused to look at him. She didn't see him as an immediate threat, but he was most certainly an obstacle.

Her eyes were fixed on the landscape passing by as they navigated the winding mountainous roads, hoping to see a city or at least some sign of civilization. Wherever they were, it was very rural.

The only indication of their whereabouts lay in the mountains themselves. They weren't the towering peaks of the Rockies in the western part of the country. They were hilly and treed and misty. She figured somewhere like the Appalachians, but in which state, she couldn't guess.

They arrived at the address and drove down a long dirt drive, ending at a small home resembling a log cabin on a vast fenced parcel of land.

It was a pretty piece of land, as land goes, flat valley acreage locked in on three sides by a not-too-distant range of mountains.

Scattered around the principal home were several outbuildings and animal pens. It looked as if someone had recently constructed this small homestead.

As they approached, she noticed a late-model black Lincoln sitting in the drive. Levi parked, exited the vehicle, and told Daria to wait for him while he checked things out. As he made his way toward the house, the front door swung open, and two men emerged onto the front deck.

Daria opened her window, hoping to hear the conversation. While she couldn't discern the words being spoken, the distinctive accents confirmed her suspicions: they were the same two men who had grabbed her. Anxiety tightened in Daria's chest as the larger of the two men approached the truck's passenger side and swung the door open. It was the Romanian. He appeared older, in his fifties, tall and imposing, towering over Levi and carrying at least forty pounds more weight.

Underneath his dark blue suit, it was apparent that he was relatively fit, though not muscular. His graying black hair was slicked back and cut short, giving her the impression of a businessman.

Although his eyes were a pale green with a blue ring around the iris, they were deep-set, which darkened their appearance. She could detect the scent of cedarwood or possibly tobacco from his aftershave. Whatever it was, it suited him.

"Levi said you took a bit of a tumble." Her insides turned, hearing his voice that close to her again, but she remained silent. "I will put you inside where you are more comfortable."

She stiffened as he put one hand behind her back and the other under her legs, gently pulling her from the vehicle. As they made their way to the house, he informed her, "This is your home now. You will live here and learn to love your husband." She stared at him incredulously.

"Your old life is behind you. Do you understand?" It was a command rather than a question.

"What about my family?" she finally spoke. "They'll be looking for me. They'll be worried. And I already have a husband—well, he will be my—"

"No!" He raised his voice. "No longer will he be your lover. This is your new life now! Your family will understand; you left for a better life."

"But—"

"No, no but. This is your life."

Tears rolled down Daria's cheeks, realizing it was no use arguing with the man.

"I will be back tomorrow. Until then, you must make no effort to leave this house. I will know," he commanded.

He placed her on the bed in the first bedroom and left her alone while he continued his conversation with Levi in the living room. Daria strained to hear their discussion.

"Put ice on her leg, then feed her and leave her alone. You will sleep in the other bedroom for now. We will speak more tomorrow. If you do not do these things, if you harm her, your deal with the judge will end. You will end. Do you understand?" His stern words resonated through the walls.

Levi responded with a quick, "Yeah, yeah." As the men left, clearly taken aback by the sudden threat.

Chapter Two

I'm What?

(2002)

Daria lay still, her gaze fixed on the blinking numbers of the digital clock across the room as evening wrapped around the house. She couldn't hear Levi; he was in the house, but she overheard him being instructed to leave her alone, so she had no idea where he was or what he was doing.

A few minutes later, she heard the front door open and close, then the sound of the truck engine turning over. Evidently, Levi was taking them seriously since she was now alone. *Great!* A perfect opportunity to escape, except for the fact she couldn't walk. When the Romanian man brought her into the house, he placed her in what she assumed was the primary bedroom. It was spacious, with a four-post queen bed, a full walk-in closet, and an ensuite. The walls were painted in a moss green color with white wood wainscoting, giving it a country cabin chic vibe.

She looked around and couldn't help but notice the room's comfort. Still, she couldn't ignore the fact that it was also her prison. Rolling over, she reached for the chain on the small lamp resting on the bedside table. With a click, it turned on, casting a warm yellowish glow, illuminating the room.

The soft light cast soft shadows on the walls, creating a subdued ambiance that did little to ease the weight of her concerns. A little anxious and heavy-hearted, she lay thinking of home and how worried her family must be, especially her grandfather.

Within the fabric of Daria's formative years, Wallace and Gillie Lovell, known affectionately as Grandpa and Gramma—were a beacon of light, her sanctuary, before she met Jet. Their absence weighed heavily on her, but she missed Jet most of all. Daria knew he was the one for her from the moment she laid eyes on him. He gave her hope, and she felt protected in his arms, like being wrapped in a warm, comfy shroud of armor that nothing could penetrate. She could sink into his arms and hide from the cruel world she came from. Oh, how she wished for those arms right now.

Jet stood towering over her by a full head. Whenever they embraced, he effortlessly lifted her off her feet, meeting her gaze with a tender kiss. His smile, that irresistibly crooked grin, seemed to ooze affection, always causing her cheeks to flush. How did he do that? Every. Single. Time. The thought brought a fleeting smile to her face, but reality soon invaded. The memory served as a bittersweet reminder of the vast distance between them. Her heart breaking as she sobbed.

When she had no more tears, she rolled over and noticed twilight had descended into darkness. She could see the stars through the window beside her bed. They blazed without the lights of a city, and she gazed at them, comparing them to the familiar stars from her home in England.

She tossed a few more times, wincing with every move, and unable to find a comfortable resting position, she tried to sit. Even worse. She fell back onto her pillow, and in her frustration, she found a few more tears.

After about an hour of silence, she heard the truck pull up. *Finally!* Levi wasn't exactly the first person she would have chosen to keep her company, but he would have to do since she was alone and a little frightened of being in a strange place. At least someone else was in the house.

Levi came in, plopped a bag of fast food on the end of the bed, then set a drink on her side table. He didn't speak until Daria said, "Thanks."

"Yeah," he replied, leaving the room and returning with a fresh ice pack. He had completed the tasks set by the Romanian and settled in the living room, turning on the TV.

As she unrolled the greasy bag, she realized she had not eaten for almost 24 hours. Inside, she found a soggy cheeseburger and cold fries, but she finished the meal without a word of complaint. Because, at that moment, anything would have tasted good. Recalling the drive there, she noted the nearest town was probably a good distance away, which didn't bode well for any attempt to escape on foot.

Early the following morning, the Lincoln pulled up. Levi was outside, exploring the grounds and outbuildings. Daria was asleep when the two men arrived at the house. The doctor knocked and then entered her room. Her eyes opened when she heard it, and she sat up, startled. *OWW!* She forgot about the knee.

It was an older gentleman in his late fifties with graying blond hair parted to one side. He was carrying a medical bag and a set of crutches in one arm. He entered the room, closing the door behind him.

His manner was not intimidating; at first glance, she thought a set of kind green eyes sat behind those black horned-rimmed glasses he wore. It was probably the first time she felt somewhat safe since this whole ordeal began. She didn't know why; maybe it was because of his grandfatherly looks, or perhaps it was just his profession.

Rubbing the sleep from her eyes, she asked, "Are you the doctor?"

His accent, not as thick as Levi's, likely due to his education, still bore a distinct southern drawl.

"Yes, I'm Dr. Reed, but everyone calls me Doc," he said with a smile. "I'm here to check your knee and, if needed, perform a physical exam."

"A physical exam? Why?"

He set his bag on the dresser and laid the crutches on the floor at the foot of the bed. Then he walked over and stood beside her, placing a specimen cup on the bedside table.

"I understand there may be some question about your being, in a family way, so to speak."

Daria's head dropped. "How do you know that?"

"Your uncle told me," he said before changing the subject. "Now, let's get you to the bathroom. I need a sample of your urine for the test."

Doc helped Daria stand, then handed her the crutches. "I can do it myself," she proclaimed.

"Well then, I'll just put the cup next to the toilet. Leave it there when you're finished."

Irritated, she said, "Yeah, okay."

When she returned, the doctor helped her back to the bed and took a look at her still-swollen knee. "This doesn't look too bad," he said. "You definitely sprained it. Keep it iced; you should feel some relief in a few days. Depending on your test results, I'll leave you some pain relievers."

He stood and walked to the bathroom, taking his bag. After poking around for a moment, he found what he needed to perform the test. Daria sat waiting anxiously, and a few minutes later, he returned with the results.

"Well, it seems congratulations are in order. You are most definitely pregnant. I'll need to do a complete exam to help determine your health and how far along you are." Doc took her temperature and blood pressure, then listened to her chest and heart and looked into her ears, nose and throat. "Next, I'll need you to undress from your waist down."

"Is this part absolutely necessary?"

"Yes, we need to be as thorough as possible since your uncle is unwilling to bring you into town just yet. We need to ensure you and your child are healthy. I'll give you some privacy and be back in a minute or two. Can you manage, or do you need help?"

"I can manage," Daria said.

When the doctor left the room, she undressed and pulled the sheet back over herself, a little freaked out about the exam. So far, Doc had been nothing but professional and kind, and she felt she could trust what he was saying.

She had only been to a gynecologist a handful of times, but those were in very clinical settings. This was not that. As she lay there staring at the ceiling, she tried to push aside her anxiety about the last part of her exam and process the news that Doc had just delivered. *I'm. Pregnant.* Calmly evaluating each word as she thought it, she questioned, *I'm pregnant?* The possibility was there; well, the odds were greater than possible, but it had been on her periphery until now when the realization hit. *OHHH SHIT–I'M PREGNANT! What am I going to do?* The weight of the news settled in, stirring a whirlwind of emotions within her.

The doctor knocked and came back in, breaking her train of thought. He proceeded to his bag, opened it, put on a pair of sterile gloves, and then pulled out a tube of lubricant. When he returned to the bed, he sat next to her, pulled the sheet down to her pelvic area, and manipulated her lower abdomen.

"Any pain or spotting?"

"No."

He pulled the sheet the rest of the way down and propped up her one good knee. Then, opening the tube of lubricant, he placed a dollop on his two fingers and said, "This may be a little cold." As he spread her legs and inserted them, he again manipulated her lower abdomen while asking questions.

"When was your last period?"

"Umm ... almost two months ago."

"Were you aware that you might be pregnant?"

"Yes. I went to the drugstore for a test, but..." Not knowing how much the doctor understood of her situation or if she could trust him, she thought, *Do I tell him what happened, or does he already know? Don't say anything until you know.*

"When, what?"

"Umm ... Well, I was interrupted and had to leave."

"I see. Does your husband know yet?"

"No, I don't think so."

"So you haven't said anything to him."

"No."

When he finished the exam, he stood, pulled the gloves off, and tossed them into a bedside trash basket.

"Well, I can't be one hundred percent sure without a sonogram, but if your dates are accurate, you should be about six or seven weeks along. Have you felt any movement yet?"

"Movement?"

"Maybe a fluttering in your lower abdomen?"

"No. Should I be?"

"No, not necessarily. It's just another indicator to help us gauge how far along you are. You should start to feel what is called the quickening around eighteen weeks or so. I'll let your uncle and husband know I need to return in a week to check your knee. We'll talk more then about what to expect. I assume this is your first?" She nodded.

"Right now, I want you to rest that knee and eat healthy foods." She noticed he looked over at the fast-food cup still sitting on the nightstand. "I'll leave some Tylenol here for pain if needed. Do you have any questions for me?"

"No." She shook her head, took a deep breath, and sighed. "But I'm sure I will."

The doctor agreed, packed up his bag, and smiled at her as he left the room. The door was left open, and she heard the men discussing the doctor's visit.

"How is she, Doc?"

"She's young and seems to be in good health. I don't foresee any complications."

"Good, good. Thank you."

"No problem. I told her I would check on her knee again next week."

"We will see to it."

The Romanian entered Daria's room as Doc left for the car. Still shocked at her news, Daria looked up to see him walk toward her.

She spoke first, "Let me guess, you're my uncle?"

"Yes, you will call me Uncle." He stood beside her. In a serious but curious voice, he said, "This news ... it is what we expected, yes?" She nodded. "You will remain here with your husband. This place is good, yes?" He smiled and nodded, holding his arms open, gesturing to her his fondness for the property he had chosen for them.

She glared up at him indignantly.

His mood fell with her lack of appreciation. "This is a good place to make a life for your child. You are fortunate. In our culture, you would have been exiled and left to fend for yourself, or worse. You would have become an outcast, and your people would have shunned you for the shame you brought to your family's name. You should be grateful!"

Daria sat confused at his chastisement of her situation. *It's not like I planned on getting pregnant, but even so, my family would never shun me. What culture? Obviously, they would be concerned for me, but make me an outcast? What is he even talking about? This guy is ... I mean ... what? Besides, Jet would never let—*She sighed in disgust.

Clearly upset with her lack of response, he continued, "I will bring the doctor for regular visits until the child is born." He turned to leave.

She interrupted his trek out of the room. "Do I at least have a change of clothes here?"

"Yes, as I said, this is your home now. Your closet is well sorted." Then he turned on his heels and left.

The more Uncle pushed his demands on her, the more determined Daria was to find a way back to her real life, to Jet, the actual father of her child. He was her first love. Her only love, after all. The man she had loved almost her whole life, who finally and amazingly loved her back. She was going to find her way back to him. She had to.

Daria scooted to the bed's edge, hearing the Lincoln drive off, and stood on her own. She grabbed the crutches, made a quick tour of the closet, then headed for the bathroom, where she started the water and sat on the tub's edge to finish undressing. Waiting for the water to heat, she sat, remembering the first time she met Jet.

Chapter Three

She's Been Mesmerized

(1990)

It was November, Thanksgiving in the US. Daria's grandparents had taken her on her first trip to England. Actually, it was her first trip anywhere. Just outside of Leeds is where Daria's great-uncle and aunt on her grandfather's side lived. Her grandparents would visit them yearly around this time and again in the early summer.

"Daria, sweetheart, why don't you come downstairs and join the family?" Gillie called from the bottom of the stairs, her great-aunt Minnie standing beside her.

Daria was hiding in the room where she slept while everyone mingled downstairs.

"She's so timid, I fear she'll miss meeting everyone," Minnie said.

The English don't celebrate Thanksgiving like Americans, so it was more of a family and friends get-together. Everyone had gathered at her great-uncle's terraced home. The aroma of roasting meat and savory herbs filled the cozy space, inviting everyone to the awaiting feast.

Daria cracked the door and could hear the laughter and chatter of the adults reminiscing, along with bursts of crying babies. She had never met this part of her family before. Although they seemed friendly, there was no one her age, and she found the house too crowded for her liking.

She hesitated, clutching her Beverly Cleary book tightly, then stepped out and peeked at her grandmother from the top of the stairs. "Can I stay up here just a bit longer? *Please*?"

Gillie sighed softly and shrugged while Minnie frowned and shook her head, both peering up the stairs. "Alright, dear. But don't stay cooped up there too long."

Daria nodded, offering a faint smile before retreating back into her room, jumping onto her bed, and curling up on top of her covers. "Okay, Socks, let's see what kind of mischief you've gotten yourself into now?"

An hour later, Gillie quietly opened the door and paused, watching her only grandchild engrossed in yet another book. Her eyes welled with a mix of joy and sorrow, realizing how much this child reminded her of her own daughter, Daria's mother. Her long, mahogany soft curls fell around her face as she read.

The scene reminded her of the times she would read to her for hours on end. Daria snuggled up in her lap, tracing her tiny fingers over her favorite words, devouring each one with wonder. She was six now, and Gillie felt a sense of relief and a little bit of pride when, at the start of school this year, Daria's teachers communicated their amazement that she was already reading.

Gillie stepped in as she snapped out of her reverie and sat beside her granddaughter.

Daria looked up at her grandmother. "Do you remember this part, Gramma?" Tracing her fingers over the pages. "You used to read it to me all the time."

Reading comforted Daria and took her little troubled mind to places she never thought she could see in real life. It was one of the few ways she could find what she thought of as some semblance of normality and how she believed happy people lived.

Gillie gently pulled the book from her hands and placed it on the bed beside them. "Yes, sweetheart, that's one of my favorites too, but dinner is ready, and everyone is waiting for you to come down." Daria nodded and grabbed her grandmother's hand as she scooted off the bed and headed down the stairs.

They took their turn walking through the small kitchen's makeshift buffet line. Gillie made her plate, letting Daria pick out all her favorites. "What would you like, dear?"

"Turkey, lots of turkey! Oh, and Mac 'n cheese, please."

"Any vegetables?"

"Do I have to?"

"No, sweetie, not today." Her grandmother smiled.

Daria beamed and pointed to the sweet potato casserole and a funny-looking bread her grandmother called Yorkshire pudding.

"Would you like gravy on that?"

Horrified, Daria screeched, "You put *gravy* on *pudding*?"

Everyone within earshot laughed at the little American girl.

Gillie, trying to hold her composure. "No, hun, it's not that kind of pudding. Here, I'll put some on the side in case you want to try it."

Still not convinced, Daria nodded as she noticed yet another family entering the home, adding to her anxiety.

Gillie led Daria to the kitchen breakfast area, where they had set up a small children's table. It was just the right size for the two toddlers already seated there, but even as small as Daria was, it was an uncomfortable fit. She sat picking at her meal, feeling lonely and out of place, watching a two-year-old and a four-year-old gobble their food.

The clatter of silverware and the distant hum of conversation surrounded her, and she wished she had her book with her. But also glad she didn't, as the youngest toddler flicked a helping of peas across the table at her. The child giggled proudly, only accentuating her loneliness amidst the chaotic joy of the toddler table.

Just then, a boy, around twelve, stomped in and plopped down in the chair in front of her. He was not happy about being in this room, especially after seeing the size of the table.

She looked up at him, mouth agape. *He's so pretty,* she thought. *Are boys allowed to be pretty?* Handsome wouldn't describe him because, in her head, she relegated the term to men who had sharper features and facial hair.

No, this boy was definitely pretty, or maybe even beautiful, with soft features and no evidence of hair on his face. Even though he was visibly upset, his cheeks were pink, his eyes were bright, and his lips were full.

The unexpected encounter brought a momentary pause to her thoughts of loneliness as she found herself mesmerized by the loose brown curls framing his boyish face. Her heart pounded in her chest. She didn't know if it was because this beautiful boy had just graced her with his presence or if she was just excited about another non-toddler sitting with her. It didn't matter, because she couldn't take her eyes off him as his mother set his plate on the table in front of him. "Sorry, darling, there's just not enough space at the grown-ups' table," his mother said apologetically before departing, leaving him to pout.

With a huff, he crossed his arms and then caught Daria's stare. "What are you looking at?"

Daria's breath caught in her throat as she lowered her gaze to the plate in front of her. *He doesn't even know me, and he already hates me.* The weight of his perceived judgment and her isolation settled in, her heart sinking as her humiliation turned into panic. She avoided making further eye contact with him as she continued to push her food around her plate.

The boy glared around the table at the children, much younger than even Daria, and noticed a tear drop onto her plate.

He groaned with an eye roll and a heavy sigh. "Ugh, don't do that. Don't cryyy!" He leaned in to get closer to her. "C'mon, little bit. I didn't mean to sound so angry. It's just that I'm not a kid anymore; I should be sitting out there with the adults, not in here with all you little ones."

Daria glared up in defiance as she wiped her face with the back of her hand and croaked, "You're not an adult ... and I'm not a baby."

He leaned back in his too small chair, crossed his arms, and gave her a long stare before proposing, "You know what, you're right. Hey, I have an idea. Let's go make our own table."

And with immediate forgiveness and a great big smile. "YEAH, let's go make our own table!"

They were now on their very own secret mission. Both children picked up their plates and snuck around the corner to the parlor where the television was. They sat down at the coffee table and found a show on the telly.

Chewing a much too large chunk of turkey that she just stabbed with her fork and crammed into her mouth. "What's your name?"

"John Elliott Thomas."

"John Elliott Thomas?" She tested the sound on her tongue, then thought for a second. "J. E. T. ... Jet, I like that."

"It's John Elliott Thomas." Emphatically repeating himself.

She giggled at his insistence. "That's too much to say. I like Jet better."

"Well, what's your name?" Still slightly annoyed.

"Daria," she sang, with a rise in pitch at the end. Then, taking another bite of food, she wiggled on the pillow he gave her to reach the table.

"That's an old lady's name. I'll call you little bit."

"Hey, that's not a name!"

"It is now." He laughed out loud.

"Okay, J. E. T!"

"Okay, Lill ... B...T." Mocking her inflection with a crooked face.

"What's a Lily B Tee?" Scrunching her nose up, not completely understanding his accent.

"Lit-ell B. T. ... means a little bitty thing. Because that's what you are."

"Take that back! I'm not lily bitty!" She was determined to show him and stood. "See!"

"Oh, yes, you are!" He laughed as he stood. "See! You only come up to here!" Holding his hand just below mid-chest right over her head. "I like that better, anyway." He sat back down.

"Like what better?" Plopping back onto her pillow, defeated.

"Lily, I like Lily better ... I'm gonna call you Lily." And with no quarrel, that became his forever name for her.

Throughout the rest of the day, they enjoyed talking and playing cards, and he even took her on a stroll to his favorite park halfway between her great-uncle's residence and his. Spending the day with Jet was a welcome escape from the chaotic gathering.

It was hard to believe that just that morning, Lily had felt overwhelmed, hiding herself away from the family gathering. But meeting

Jet changed everything. Despite their slightly awkward introduction, he listened to her with genuine interest, making her feel understood in a way no one else did. With him, she felt like more than just a kid among adults, finding comfort and connection amidst the bustling activity of the day.

Later, almost everyone had said their goodbyes and headed home as the evening set in. Only Jet and his parents remained. Lily's grandmother, great-aunt, and Jet's mum sat in the kitchen after cleaning up, sipping a glass of wine while the men gathered in the garden to smoke their cigars. Jet and Lily were back in the parlor watching the telly. Lily crawled up on the couch next to Jet.

"Did you have fun today?" Jet asked, glancing over at Lily with a smile.

"I did." Returning a bright smile. "Thank you for showing me the park. The troll bridge was my favorite part. Can we go there again before I leave?"

"Sure, I'm there most Saturday mornings playing football."

"So, Saturday morning then?" He nodded. It was a date, they both agreed as Jet turned his attention back to the television flipping through the channels to find his favorite show.

As Jet watched Top of the Pops, it wasn't long before Lily drifted, her head bobbing. Jet caught her as she fell toward him and rested her head on his lap until her grandfather came in and put her to bed.

(2002)

Daria smiled at the memory. Then she wept as a wave of sadness washed over her. Worried about the fate of herself and her unborn child, she got in the tub, allowing the warm water to embrace her, loosening her aching muscles and providing a momentary sanctuary as she grappled with the weight of her circumstances. Her mind was now racing, considering her next steps. More determined than ever, she contemplated her escape.

Chapter Four

Held Breath

(2002)

A week slipped by, and Daria focused on the gradual healing of her leg. She couldn't do much until then, especially without knowing exactly where she was.

Then, one evening, the static-laden voice of a local newscaster filtered through the speakers of their old rabbit-eared television. Between the flickers of the screen and the snippets of weather reports and local happenings, she caught mention of the mountains of eastern Kentucky. As the pieces fell into place, Daria realized that these remote, towering landscapes she'd been staring at through the window were her current confines, nestled deep in the heart of Appalachia. Finally, a firm location.

The following morning, a car pulled up in the drive. It was the Lincoln. Uncle had brought Doc by to check on Daria. It was still early, and the room was dimly lit as they pushed open the front door. A wave of stale air hit them, along with the sight of Levi sprawled out on the couch, drunk and snoring loudly. He had propped his boots, caked in mud, up on the coffee table. Uncle, with a look of disgust, strode over to him, knocking both feet off the table with one swift kick. Levi grumbled but didn't wake.

Daria was out of sight, but they could hear her faint breathing from the bedroom, her leg propped up on a pillow. The knocking thud sounds of movement reached her ears, rousing her from her sleep. The throbbing pain in her leg served as a reminder of her vulnerability, and she cautiously shifted her attention to the commotion outside the bedroom.

Doc walked in and stood by her side. "Good morning. Sorry to wake you this early, but I have rounds today, and you're the furthest out. I told you I would be back this week." Daria sat up and nodded, remembering the conversation. "How is your knee today?"

"Fine, I guess. I have been able to stand on it without crutches for short periods."

"Good. Now, how are you?" He gave her a suspicious look.

"I'm okay," she lied.

They heard more commotion coming from the living room as the front door opened and then a definite *WHOMP* in the front yard. Levi yelled, "What the hell, man?"

Uncle raised his voice and said, "This behavior is unacceptable. You have a wife and child to care for now!"

Levi barked back, "I didn't bargain for no kid when I agreed to this deal."

"Young man, this is the deal; if you do not like it, I will send you back to the judge for sentencing. Would that be good?"

They heard another scuffle, and Levi yelled again, "A'right, A'right!" Then it became quiet.

Both Doc and Daria sat in a quiet state of shock and curiosity as Doc looked out her front window to see both men walking toward one of the outbuildings. Finally, he looked down at Daria and nodded toward the living room. "Is this a regular occurrence?"

"Oh, that? Pfft. Yep, ever since I met him."

"How long have you been married?"

"About a week."

"How long have you known him?"

"About a week."

Doc looked confused and pointed at Daria's belly. "So, this is not his child?"

Crap! Big mouth. She caught herself, not thinking; the realization of her slip hung in the air, having just blurted out information so nonchalantly. She thought for a second, looked up at Doc, and decided that it was now or never if she was going to trust someone to help her. Then she asked, "Doctor-patient confidentiality?"

"Of course."

Whispering, "Doc, can you get a message to my family? I'm not supposed to be here. They kidnapped me and brought me here. I need to get back home."

"Where is home?"

"England." She ripped a page out of the book on her bedside table and asked for his pen. "Here is my family's number." She handed him the torn paper. "Can you call them and tell them where I am?"

"Of course, but shouldn't I call the sheriff first and tell them?"

"No, they may be in on it. It was a sheriff that gave us our marriage license and IDs and told Levi to bring us here."

"What about your uncle?"

"He's not my uncle; I never met him before last week. He and another man grabbed me from the drugstore. That's why I didn't get the pregnancy test then. They drugged me, and I woke up here in the States."

"This is quite a fantastic story." He shook his head and wiped his brow with his handkerchief. "This is a small town; things like that don't happen here."

"Can you do this for me?" she begged.

"Yes ... yes, of course."

The front door opened. Doc put the paper in his coat pocket. Levi walked in, cursing under his breath, and stomped into the kitchen. Uncle walked into the bedroom and asked, "Are we finished?"

"Uh ... Yes, we were just finishing up. I think we should get some prenatal blood work going in a few days."

Smart! Coming up with an excuse to come back. Thanks, Doc!

"Yes, that will be fine," said Uncle. He gestured towards the door, looking at Daria and then the doctor.

"Thank you, Doc!" Daria said. He nodded nervously, and then the two men left.

Days passed with no visit from Doc. Daria wondered if he was able to contact her family. She was finally walking on her leg without crutches and moving freely around the house, and her sense of isolation deepened as another week passed.

Levi, absorbed in the steady rhythm of farm life, rarely crossed paths with her except when hunger called. It was almost as if he was afraid of her. Daria attributed it to the physical confrontation with Uncle during the barn meeting, following Levi's drunken sprawl on the couch.

Levi's demands for evening meals and his expectations of her to jump at his command revealed the type of wife he expected her to be—quiet and obedient. She went along with it begrudgingly, figuring she'd better play the part for now, as she hoped for news from the outside.

Over the next couple of weeks, they had settled into a routine, and the monotony of the evening unfolded with a predictable cadence. When Levi finished dinner, he would retire to the recliner with a fifth of whiskey that had become his steady companion and drink himself to sleep. Daria, however, would try to lose herself in a book, as the TV cast faint shadows from her door.

With each passing day, Daria became more and more desperate for information. If Doc was able to contact them, she thought she needed to stay and wait for them to rescue her, but if not, she would still need to devise a plan of escape.

It was late one afternoon, and after several weeks of waiting, Uncle finally showed up with Doc. She ran to the window when she heard the car drive up and watched as they parked. *Wait, that's not Doc! Who's this?*

When a woman carrying a medical case stepped out of the car, Daria greeted her at the door and ushered her inside. Uncle told the woman to set up in the main bedroom and pointed her in the right direction. The woman nodded in acknowledgment and made her way to the designated room. Once the woman had left, Uncle turned to Daria. "Did you really think I would not discover your little deception?" His tone betrayed a mix of anger and frustration.

Daria's heart stopped. *He knows.* "What do you mean?"

"You will not do that again," he said sternly. "Your family is no longer looking for you. They now believe you have run away to find yourself a new life. This is true, yes?"

Daria dropped into the chair behind her. "That's not true, they would never believe that—Jet would never believe that!" she shouted as she broke into a sob. "Why are you doing this? What have I ever done to you?" She paused in thought and then questioned, "Did my stepfather make you do this!? If he told you he'd pay you, he won't, ya know! He'll betray you! Just like everyone else, he—Please, just let me go home. I promise I won't tell anyone— anything, I swear!"

"It is done, child. No more will you try to contact your family. If you do, they will end up like Doc."

"What did you do to Doc!" she screamed.

"Calm yourself. You will harm the child." He pointed to the bedroom and said, "This is your new doctor. She will care for you from now on. She will perform the needed tests." Daria continued to sob as he demanded, "Now, go to her." Inconsolable, Daria rose from her seat, her sobs echoing in the room.

She made her way to the bedroom. Reaching the door, her trembling hand grasped the handle as she walked through. Her frustration transformed into defiance as she spun around, shooting Uncle a hateful glare, and with one final rebellious act, she slammed the door shut with all her might; the force of it reverberating through the walls of her home.

Daria stood staring at the closed door when the new doctor asked her to come and sit down on the bed. "I need to take your blood for testing."

Fabulous, another Romanian. There would be no doctor-patient confidentiality with this one, she figured. Daria looked up at her and nodded. She was a tall, slender woman, almost too thin. Nothing about this woman read doctor; a more likely description would have been runway model.

This woman's lips were full, painted in a vibrant violet-red, adding a striking contrast to her sharp bob haircut that grazed just below her ears. Her features were narrow and pale for her ethnicity, and she spoke with a heavily accented voice, even more pronounced than Uncle's. Daria, giving in for the sake of her unborn child, sat and extended her arm for the tests, silently allowing the doctor to proceed with her work, her eyes fixed on the woman's every move.

After the doctor finished the exam and they left, Levi came into the house, having heard the commotion, where he found Daria sobbing into her pillow.

He said, "Hey girl, they got to you too, I see." As he leaned on her bedroom door frame.

"What?" she said, sitting up.

"This is the deal we made. Now it looks like we're stuck with each other."

With tears streaming down her face yet again, her eyes darted over to Levi, and in a fit of anger, she bit back. "I didn't make any deal with anyone! I have a family and a boyfriend who loves me. He is the father of this child! Not you!"

Levi snarked back, "Not accordin' to yer uncle. Yer mine now, along with that brat yer carrying, and ya migh' as well get used to it." And with that, he twisted around and walked back outside.

Her heart pounded in her chest, each beat a painful reminder of the uncertainty that loomed over her future, and with no understanding of why, Daria plopped back down, burying her face into her pillow, and screamed as loud as she could. Eventually, out of tears and exhausted, she gave in to sleep.

Chapter Five

Going Home

(1991)

It was Saturday morning, late spring in 1991, and Daria knew where Jet would be.

Over time, Jet's parents developed a close bond with Daria's grandparents, having met them through her great-uncle and aunt. They eagerly encouraged Jet to spend time with her whenever they visited.

At the local park, Jet met up with some of his friends, and naturally, Daria wasn't far behind.

During her first visit to England, Daria's heart danced with joy as she and Jet formed an instant connection. She believed they were now the best of friends, and the feeling seemed mutual as they spent every moment together during this subsequent trip. Daria cherished each second spent in Jet's company, clinging to him like a shadow wherever he roamed.

"Oy, who's the little bird following you?" Reggie, one of the boys, joked.

Jet looked behind him and furrowed his brows. "Yeah, that's Daria. She's visiting from the US. I guess I'm kinda babysitting." He scratched his head. "Her grandparents are friends with my mum and dad."

Daria stepped beside him and grabbed his hand. "Hi, my English name is Lily." The boy looked at Jet, confused. Jet sighed and shook his head. "Long story." And he left it at that.

Another boy named Ronny ran up to them. "Hey, are you here to play some football or what? We need another player."

Jet looked down at her. "Do you mind if I play?"

"Can I watch?"

"Sure, but don't go running off or anything," She shook her head, and at that, he let go of her hand and ran out to the field.

Lily turned, searching for a comfortable patch of grass to watch the boys play. However, not understanding the game, she quickly grew bored and began wandering around the field, never straying too far from Jet's sight.

When the game was over, Jet ran to the patch of grass, where Lily finally came to rest and collapsed beside her. She had been collecting flowers while he played and had a full fist of grasses and flowering weeds in her little hand. She was very proud of her collection and presented Jet with the bouquet as he sat up.

"What's this?"

"Our wedding bouquet," she said proudly.

"Wedding bouquet? So, we're getting married?" Jet laughed.

"Yes ... not today, but one day when we grow up."

"Lily, I'm too old for you. By the time you grow up, I'll already be married."

She ignored his argument. "When we get married," Daria declared, rising to her feet, "I want a bouquet just like this one and a pretty dress." She moved behind him, encircling her arms around his neck, and leaning over his shoulder, she smashed a long, humming kiss onto his cheek.

Jet's face turned bright red, noticing the boys across the field watching and laughing. Then, with a heavy sigh, he unhitched her arms, got up, and grabbed her hand. "Come on, Lily, let's go home."

(2002)

Daria's eyes blinked open. Yawning and stretching, then rubbing her swollen eyes, she looked around at her surroundings, only to see her new prison and realize nothing had changed. She sat up, weeping into her hands. *I can't stay here anymore; I have to get out of here.* Desperate to get back home to her family and the man she loved. *I don't care how far I have to walk.* She got up, quietly packed a small bag with just the bare essentials and hid it under her bed. She'd leave tonight after dinner.

As Levi's snores echoed through the house, Daria seized the moment, snatching her bag and slipping out into the moonlit night. Each step down the rugged and never-ending driveway quickened her pulse, anticipation coursing through her veins. The darkness cloaked her movements as she made her getaway, her heart pounding with the thrill of freedom. She could almost taste the sweetness of Jet's kiss and feel the comforting warmth of her family's embrace enveloping her.

With each stride, she felt the pull of home grow more powerful, more tangible, and hoping to hitch a ride into town, the expectation of an eventual escape more certain. But just as she reached the road and turned onto the blacktop, Uncle's Lincoln materialized beside her, shattering her hopes with its unwelcome presence.

Caught off guard, she stared blankly through the passenger-side window, her mind racing with questions. *How the hell did he know?* And—How had he found her so quickly? Uncertainty held her in place, hesitating for a moment longer.

The window rolled down. "Get in!" his command echoed, leaving her with no other choice.

He drove her back to the house. "Where do you think you're going?"

She didn't answer.

"Your life is here now; I have told you, you must not leave. Did you think you could just walk out of here? There is no one on this road for many miles. You are in the middle of nowhere, and it is night. Very large animals come out to feed at night. You put yourself and your child in danger! Do I need to prove I am serious?"

"Please," Daria pleaded through tears, "Please just let me go home."

The car rolled to a stop in front of the house, and Daria stepped out, her movements filled with a mixture of defiance and resignation. With a forceful slam, she closed the car door behind her; the sound echoing through the once tranquil homestead, waking the animals.

As Uncle maneuvered the Lincoln to leave, he lowered the window, his voice carrying a chilling warning. "The next time you stray, I will bring you your grandfather's ear. Do you understand?" Stunned into silence by his threat, she simply nodded, watching as the car disappeared into the night. Turning back toward the house, she couldn't shake the feeling of dread that settled in the pit of her stomach.

As she crawled under the covers, thoughts of Jet flooded her mind, his absence weighing heavily on her heart. The shattered hopes of their reunion left her feeling hollow. In an effort to calm herself, she tried to redirect her thoughts to the time she spent with her grandparents in England, cherishing those precious memories.

But thoughts of her parents, or rather, her stepfather, seemed to dominate her thoughts this night. The unwelcome intrusion of his face brought with it a wave of anxiety, stirring up memories of past threats and unresolved trauma. The threat Uncle made tonight only served to reinforce those haunting memories, echoing the venomous words her stepfather had continually spat at her and her mother.

Chapter Six

Why Do We Hurt This Way (1983-1990)

In the heart of Athens, Georgia, nestled on the banks of the Oconee River, a picturesque southern town adorned with Antebellum architecture and oak-lined streets, sixteen-year-old Joanna Lovell's story unfolded, laying the foundation for Daria Daniels' own tale.

It all began with a whirlwind romance the summer before her senior year—the kind that inspired passion and dreams that last forever. As a young woman with bright eyes that could ignite a room, Joanna wore her long mahogany locks in a braid pulled over one shoulder. She possessed an exotic beauty that turned heads and captured hearts, including a boy she met at a city bus stop, sitting all alone and in need of help.

Marik Daniels was a vagabond of sorts whose unconventional lifestyle only added to his allure. Their short-lived romance led to a moment of youthful recklessness, and soon Joanna found herself pregnant and abandoned. Her heart was broken, and her dreams shattered in the wake of impending motherhood, marking the beginning of a journey that spiraled into eventual despair.

At just seventeen, Joanna lived with her parents when her daughter Daria Daniels entered the world. Her cries echoed through the hospital, a precursor to the restless spirit she would carry for months.

Doctors attributed her persistent wails to colic, but to Joanna, they were nothing short of deafening.

Instead of returning to school, she forged ahead, opting for a GED and a job as a zero operator for Southern Bell. The overnight shift was her preferred choice, but she would work any available hours as long as they kept her away from home. Joanna's young soul, still burning for the spirit of the 1980s teenage experience, danced between the responsibilities of adulthood and the allure of freedom. The appeal of parties and newfound friendships took precedence, and sometimes, on evenings she didn't have to work; she would stay out all night, leaving Daria in the loving care of her grandparents, Wallace and Gillie Lovell.

Daria grew into a bright-eyed toddler who brought joy and mischief into their lives. Her grandfather commented to a friend one evening that as soon as they grabbed one little hand away from danger, the other was already reaching for something else. But they loved her dearly and were thankful for their time with her.

The passage of time and Daria's growth marked a significant change in Joanna's life as well. Like countless other young adults facing similar circumstances, Joanna felt confined and did not relish living under her parents' rule.

Seeking liberation, Joanna moved her and Daria into a small apartment. Embracing her newfound independence, she was drawn to the allure of bad boys and the thrill of new beginnings, bouncing from one boyfriend to another.

Enter Robert Reynolds. Rob was the embodiment of your typical narcissist. A troubled soul perpetually entangled in a web of illegal activities. Athens, being a college football town, Rob engaged in everything from drug dealing to handling stolen goods and even betting on underground games, always finding himself at the center of trouble.

His sharp jawline and piercing blue eyes hinted at a rugged charm and told stories of a life lived on the edge. Sporting a shaved head and tattoos that ran over his scalp, neck, and down his arms also suggested a man not to be trifled with. He believed himself to be an influential figure and leader among his, for lack of a better term, associates. But truth be told, he was pretty low on the totem pole of the local criminal hierarchy.

His initial good behavior convinced Joanna's parents that he would be a positive influence on her. Hoping for stability, they welcomed Rob into their daughter's life, unaware of the darkness that lurked beneath his facade.

After Joanna and Rob exchanged vows just before Daria turned three, they moved into a little cottage outside Athens. Their union marked the beginning of a tumultuous journey marred by abuse and addiction.

For Daria, the years that followed were a blur of chaos and violence, her innocence shattered by the echoes of her parents' conflicts.

Despite her grandparents' pleas, Joanna remained ensnared in Rob's grasp, unwilling to sever ties with her abuser. Her natural beauty was now waning, and she appeared to them as a thinning waif with drawn cheeks and deep circles under her eyes. Wallace and Gillie were worried for her and Daria's safety. They could see the changes in her ability to care for herself and the child.

The turning point for Wallace came with a single phone call—a desperate plea for help from a terrified five-year-old.

On this particular occasion, Rob was angry because Joanna was late getting home from work. Accusations of infidelity rang through the home; of course, Joanna denied it and tried to explain there was an accident on the road ahead of her, but he didn't want to hear it.

It didn't matter whether she was telling the truth when he got like this; he had been inconvenienced, and someone was going to pay. Rob's rage erupted into violence; he needed something, or someone, to hit. And so he did. He struck Joanna with his fist so hard that her head slammed against the corner of the wall. She collapsed onto the floor, unconscious and bleeding.

Rob saw the blood pooling around his wife. Daria's cries pierced the night as she ran over to help her mother.

He came after her. "Do you want some of this too!?"

Daria ignored his threat and dropped to her knees, grabbing her mother by the shoulders and shaking her. "Mama! Mama, please wake up!"

Rob stomped over, grabbed Daria's ponytail, and slung her across the room. He yelled as she hit the glass coffee table, "Stay away from her! That bitch deserved it."

He paused, his mind racing as he glanced at the shambles before him. Rob figured, this time, he was going to jail for sure. The sight of Daria crying amidst the shards of broken glass and Joanna unconscious and bleeding sparked a moment of clarity, twisted as it was. He realized he needed a way out, a story so convincing that no one would question his innocence.

The idea hit him like a bolt of lightning. A home invasion. Yes, that would work. It was simple, believable, and, most importantly, it would shift any suspicion away from him. A smirk fell upon his face. He would manipulate the narrative. It would be easy, especially against the word of a traumatized child and a woman too scared to contradict him.

With a sinister plan forming, Rob didn't hesitate. He strode through the chaos he had created, his boots crunching on glass, and grabbed his keys off the kitchen counter. Without a backward glance at the devastation he'd left in his wake, he stepped out into the night; the door slamming behind him.

As he walked to his car, parked under the dim light of a streetlamp, his mind was already weaving the web of lies he would tell. He started the engine; the sound slicing through the quiet neighborhood.

He needed an alibi, something solid, something ironclad. And he knew just where to find it.

Daria waited to hear Rob's car leave before reaching for the phone and dialing the only number she had memorized—her grandparents'.

Wallace picked up the phone to a cacophony of sobs and gasps. The voice on the other end was small, filled with fear.

"Daria, honey, is that you? What's wrong?" Wallace's voice was steady, but his heart raced with concern.

"Grandpa ... it's bad! Mama and Rob ... they were fighting again!" Daria's words stumbled over each other, barely coherent through her crying.

"Slow down, sweetheart. Tell Grandpa what happened," Wallace coaxed gently. Gillie stood close, listening with worry.

"Rob ... he was yelling ... and then he hit Mama. I'm scared, Grandpa! I don't know what to do!" Her voice, a mix of fear and confusion, lost in the storm of adult anger.

Wallace's grip on the phone tightened. "Listen to me, Daria. Are you okay?"

"I don't think so. Mama's bleeding, too. She won't wake up Grandpa."

"Is Rob there?"

"No, he left."

With a sigh of relief. "I want you to stay there, okay? Stay right where you are. Can you do that for me?"

Daria sniffled, her voice almost a whisper in the darkness. "Yes, Grandpa. But I'm really scared."

"I know you are, honey. But you're brave, too. You're the bravest little girl I know. Someone will be there soon; I will be there soon."

"You promise, Grandpa?"

"I promise, sweetheart."

"Okay, Grandpa."

He could hear her breathing slow as he reassured her. "Good girl. I need to hang up so I can call for help, okay? Remember, I love you very much."

"I love you too, Grandpa."

Wallace hung up the phone. His next action was swift: he dialed emergency services, and with a trembling hand, he handed the phone to Gillie so she could fill them in as he raced out the door. The fear in Daria's voice provoked a fierce determination to get to her and his daughter, no matter what it took.

The scene at the little cottage on the outskirts of Athens became a whirlwind of activity as emergency services arrived. Amid the chaos, Wallace pushed through, his heart heavy with worry for his daughter and granddaughter. Unsure of what he would find, he was ready to face it head-on.

As the dust settled and Joanna and Daria were whisked away to the safety of the hospital, the true extent of their injuries unfolded. Joanna's recovery required a two-week period in the hospital for treatment and months of observation. In contrast, Daria's injuries, though severe, didn't need prolonged medical care. She endured the immediate pain of a dislocated shoulder; the injury compounded by the need for stitches. The glass from the shattered coffee table had cut into her arm, marking her skin with a tangible reminder of the night's horror.

Joanna, overwhelmed with guilt over what had happened, promised Daria it would never happen again. Love, fear, and the struggle for survival undeniably shaped their bond, with events like these overshadowing Joanna's efforts to protect her daughter from harm. Though Joanna's love for Daria never wavered, her inability to escape Rob's control left their relationship strained and filled with uncertainty.

In the aftermath of that fateful night, Daria's grandparents had to take decisive action. The decision to intervene wasn't made lightly. But the safety and well-being of their granddaughter stood paramount. Filing for custody was their first move, a legal step towards ensuring Daria's protection. The paperwork, the court dates and the endless waiting tested their resolve, but the thought of Daria living in a safe, nurturing environment spurred them on.

Joanna tried to fight her parents and the courts for months. However, the accumulation of past evidence and her parents' testimony left the courts with no alternative but to decree a shift in custody. In the end, it was Joanna's unwavering loyalty to Rob that ultimately severed the fragile bonds between mother and daughter.

On the day of their last court date, Rob lurked outside with a chilling determination. He trailed Wallace to their car, where Daria anxiously waited with her grandmother. With a venomous glare, he unleashed a flood of threats, vowing to hunt them down, obliterate them, and reclaim Daria by any means necessary. To him, she was nothing more than a possession he refused to hand over, mirroring the possessive grip he maintained over Joanna.

Hearing the commotion, Daria begged her grandparents not to let him take her. After consulting with the attorneys, they suggested a cooling-off period, getting out of town for a while. So, they took Daria on a Thanksgiving trip they had earlier planned to England—a temporary reprieve from the shadows that haunted their lives.

Daria's grandparents became her steadfast guardians, their love serving as her anchor in a sea of uncertainty. Unfortunately, they felt compelled to homeschool Daria in order to shield her from the spector of Rob's threats that continued to loom over them. As she grew older, the scars of her past only deepened, and despite their unwavering support, Daria struggled to find the strength to navigate the turbulent waters of her future.

Chapter Seven

Little Girl's Dream

(1993)

In the crisp embrace of an English autumn, Daria's grandparents allowed her to stay with her great-uncle and aunt for an extended period so they could travel to Italy. They wanted Daria to come with them, but she begged them to let her stay until they returned.

"Darling, are you sure you wouldn't rather come to Italy with us?" Daria's grandmother asked, her voice laced with concern as they stood in the living room, surrounded by the warm glow of the fireplace.

Daria, her eyes wide with a mix of excitement and pleading, clutched her grandmother's hand. "Please, Gramma, can I stay here with Uncle Abe and Aunt Minnie? I promise I'll be good."

Wallace exchanged a look with Gillie. His eyebrows raised in a silent question. After a moment, he sighed, a smile breaking across his face. Gillie smiled and rolled her eyes, knowing he could never say no to her. "Alright, Daria. If it means that much to you, you can stay. But promise you'll keep up with your schoolwork."

Daria jumped with joy, wrapping her arms around her grandparents. "I promise! Thank you, thank you!"

During Daria's stay, her great-aunt's sister passed away, and they had to leave town for the funeral. Jet's parents offered to take care of the eight-year-old for the week.

The next day, Daria found herself in the kitchen with her great-aunt Minnie, the scent of freshly baked scones lingering in the air. She looked up into her great-aunt's eyes and noticed they were red and wet.

"Daria, my dear," Aunt Minnie began, her voice trembling slightly, "I'm afraid we have to go to Bristol for a few days. My sister has passed away, and we need to attend her funeral."

Daria's heart sank, her excitement dimming at the thought of her aunt's loss. "I'm so sorry, Auntie," she whispered, moving closer to offer a comforting hug.

Minnie squeezed her gently. "Thank you, darling. But don't you worry? Jet's parents have offered to take care of you while we're gone. You'll have a great time with them."

Daria nodded, a mix of nervousness and anticipation stirring within her. "I get to stay with Jet?" she asked, a hopeful glimmer in her eyes.

Minnie smiled with a spark of recognition. "Yes, love. I'm sure you and Jet will have lots of fun together."

In the quiet of her second night with them, Lily became restless while she slept in their guest room. Bathed in the soft glow of moonlight filtering through the curtains, she tossed and turned, then tugged and fought, her small voice softly crying out, struggling against her unseen foes.

"No! Stop! I don't wanna go!" Tears fell onto her pillow.

This would be the first time Jet would experience the turmoil of Daria's nightmares, an introduction to the unseen scars that tormented her sleep.

It was always the same core fear-based dream, although it morphed through countless versions. This one, however, starts when Rob finds her at the park where she and Jet liked to play. He snuck up behind her from the bushes surrounding the playground while Jet was playing football on the field.

She was enjoying the large industrial swings made of metal and heavy gauge chains with vinyl strap seats. They reminded her of the school swings near her home. Her grandmother and she would go for a walk in the mornings. Daria would watch the children swing and silently wish she could go to school and play with the other kids.

Daria was making her best effort to swing as high as possible, her laughter bubbling up with that giddy sensation of nearly flying off the seat. The breeze, unusually warm for England at this time of year, caressed her face as she swooped down. As she arched upward, the world briefly turned upside down.

Her body left the swing as Rob grabbed her mid-air and yanked her out of the seat. "I got you!" His voice was a mixture of laughter and triumph. She screamed as loud as she could, but no sound escaped her lips as she was carried away into an uncertain fate.

The grip of panic tightened as she tried to kick and fight, but she couldn't escape his grasp. The people in the park seemed oblivious to the unfolding struggle, and her growing distance away from the crowd heightened her fears. Was he going to kill her this time?

Daria woke up crying and ran into Jet's room. She stood at the foot of his bed, watching him sleep.

"Jet ... Jet, please wake up ... Jet," she whispered. When he didn't respond, she turned back to go to her room but stopped at the door, looking both ways down the hall. The darkness was too suffocating for her to face alone. Turning away, she attempted to brush away the tears that clung stubbornly to her cheeks. Then, gently, she crawled onto the foot of his bed, and through quiet sobs, she eventually gave way to sleep once more. Simply being close to him helped to quell her fear.

Daria believed Jet protected her from the world. He was the one who always stood up for her when the bully boys at the park teased her about being a yank. Sometimes, when she did something wrong, he would take the blame for it, or at least blame it on the fact he was older and should have corrected her, sheltering her from punishment.

Jet woke up to find her curled up and shivering. Quickly, he draped his blanket over her and rushed downstairs to his mum.

"Daria's family warned us about her nightmares," she said immediately, understanding his concern. "She must have gotten scared and come into your room."

"Scared? What does she have to be afraid of? She gets everything she wants. Her grandparents take her on long vacations. She gets homeschooled, and—"

"Son, your Lily hasn't had the life you think she's had. She is a scared little girl who's survived both physical and emotional abuse most of her young life at the hands of those dregs her mother would bring home, but even worse—" Her expression shifting as Jet observed the anger building within her, manifesting in a tight shake of her head. "The things her stepfather did—" She considered her next confession and then decided. "Son, I won't tell you everything they told me, but just to give you some insight into the severity of what she's been through ... you've seen those pox marks on her shoulder and back?" He nodded. "Those aren't from chicken pox. Those are burns from cigarettes."

"Oh God." A wave of nausea washed over him. Jet leaned back against the counter in shock at what he had just heard, dropping his head, the room seeming to spin as he absorbed this detail of Lily's past.

"It's why her grandparents brought her to England. For a bit of a respite, if you will. Do they spoil her a little? Yes, but I think it's to make up for it all. That man they call a stepfather keeps harassing and threatening them as if the poor thing hasn't been through enough. She's afraid he will steal her back and hurt her again."

He now understood her behavior around him. She wasn't just being a pest, clinging to him constantly. To her, he was a safety net, a source of protection, enveloping her in an invisible shield of security that he unknowingly provided. Guilt washed over him for all the times he had told her to stop pestering or following him.

"What's the matter, Love?" his mother said, touching his shoulder.

"I didn't know, Mum." He looked up at her with a mix of grief and awe. "She's so little and sweet, and I've been ... how could someone do that?"

"Oh, Hun, how could you have known? There are sick people in this world, John. You just never know. This is supposed to be the place where she can come to forget all of that. But sometimes it doesn't matter how far you run from your problems; they always seem to have a way of finding you."

He wiped one cheek, trying to hide the mix of emotions he harbored as he looked back at her. Mum pulled him close and hugged him tight for a long moment, then kissed him on his forehead and said, "Why don't you go wake her up for some breakfast?" He nodded and turned to head for his room, but Lily was already standing in the doorway. A single tear traced down her cheek, and she turned and ran out of the house. Jet took off after her.

Frantically, she rushed down the street, her bare feet stinging against the cold pavement, desperate to reach the park and seek refuge beneath the old stone troll bridge. That's where Jet found her, sitting with her head buried in her knees, arms clutching them.

When he got to her, he heard her sniffle. "Lily? Are you okay?"

She looked up at him, face pink and wet from tears. "Is he coming here? Mum said he would find me. I won't go back, Jet. I can't go back! I'd rather die..." she cried, shaking her head back into her arms.

"Lily, don't talk like that," he urged firmly, touching her shoulder.

"At least I would know how it happens." She looked up at him with resolve.

"Lily," he pleaded.

"Are you going to make me go back?"

Kneeling in front of her, he said, "Of course not!" He spoke with a harsh resolve and then softened a bit. "We would never send you back to him! Lily, if it ever came to that—if he showed up here, I would take you away and hide you myself. I promise."

With her arms outstretched, he reached her, settling onto the ground, legs crossed in front of him. Reaching out, he welcomed her. Climbing into his lap, she wrapped her arms around him tightly, burying her face into his chest. He returned the hug, both arms comforting her and gently stroking her back as he rested his head on hers. The silent exchange of comfort continued as she sought refuge in his embrace. No words passed between them for a while. When her grip relaxed, he asked, "Are you hungry?"

Glancing up at him, her eyes no longer teary and her heartbeat steadier; she heard her tummy growl. She giggled and nodded. "Yes."

"C'mon, you don't have any shoes on. I'll give you a piggyback ride back to the house?"

She hopped up, waited for him to get into position, and then jumped on his back. They plodded home. Lily clung to his neck, her arms wrapped tightly, snuggling close as a profound stillness flowed through her. At that moment, he had proven his love for her, promising to be the champion she needed. She knew, with him, she was safe.

(2002)

Daria rolled out of bed, unable to sleep as memories flooded her mind. Hoping to redirect her restless thoughts, she picked up a book and trudged into the living room. Sitting on the couch, book in her lap, she attempted to read, but fatigue eventually overcame her, and she dozed off.

Chapter Eight

He Takes Me Away

(2002)

As the weeks rolled by, Daria's apprehension about her uncle's threats toward her family lingered. But Daria found some comfort in helping Levi with the daily tasks of keeping their little homestead afloat. Gathering eggs, tending to the chickens, mucking out stalls, and replenishing hay became her daily rituals. She loved working with the animals. Despite her city upbringing, she developed a fondness for working alongside them, finding comfort in their silent companionship. They had become her pro-tem group of counselors she could confide in. She thought that if she had to be imprisoned, at least she had them.

The Stratton barn housed a milk cow named Daisy, a horse named Rocket, and two goats named Bonnie and Clyde because they were always getting into something. On the other side, a chicken coop, fenced and covered, housed about twenty chickens. Levi put his foot down when she tried naming all of them, but she named them anyway.

Daria picked up a white chicken. "You look like a snowball ... I'll call you Snowy." She set her down and picked up another as Levi walked out of the barn and over to her.

Levi sighed in exasperation. "Girl! I told you to stop naming the animals. One of these days, yer gonna have to eat them ... then what er ya gonna do?"

She shot Levi a rebellious sneer and covered the chicken's head where she supposed its ears would be. "Don't listen to him; we would never eat you!"

Levi rolled his eyes with a smirk. "Just make sure you're not naming the rooster 'Colonel Sanders' or something, a'right? It may give me Ideas!"

Amidst the daily grind of chores, Daria found moments of respite when her mind wandered back home and to Jet. She wondered if he, too, was lost in thoughts of her. She missed him so much that the mere thought of him made her chest ache and her throat burn. The pain was unspeakable. *Is this my heart breaking?* She knew it was.

On better days, while working, she would hum one of her favorite songs. The words and the melody comforted her and gave her at least some solace. Over and over, she would sing or hum the tune.

Levi came around the corner one afternoon as she was sweeping off the front porch deck. "What's that song you keep singing? Don't you know no other songs?"

"I know a lot of other songs, but this one is my favorite. It reminds me of home."

"You mean him."

"Don't you have someone you loved Levi? Isn't there anyone you want to get back to? Family? Friends?"

He didn't answer. "Do you have any idea what it's like to be torn away from that? I don't know if he's okay ... If he's looking for me, or my family, for that matter. Are they still looking, or am I to believe Uncle?" She paused and almost under her breath, but loud enough for him to hear her, she said, "I will never believe Uncle." She left it at that and continued to sweep.

Levi smirked back. "I had a girl once. Broke my heart..." He wiped his forehead with the back of his arm. "Never again..." He walked off, mumbling, "Only good fer one thing anyway..."

Daria stopped sweeping and spoke up. "And what's that? Cooking?"

He looked back, gave her a snarky look, and waved her off.

She half-smiled, a flicker of satisfaction crossing her face as she sensed his annoyance. Under her breath, as she resumed sweeping, she muttered, "That better be all they're good for." Her voice, barely audible, she continued to sing her song while she finished her task and let her mind wander.

Fought the tide, but now I see
The truth that's hidden deep in me
Your touch, your laugh, so wild and free
It's you I need, it's you I need
Caught in love, no more denying
Heart's on fire, there's no more hiding
Words are forming, can't keep quiet
Caught in love, my soul's ignited

Chapter Nine

Fragile Wings

(1994)

Amidst the backdrop of the '90's music scene, Grunge was taking its leave as bands that leaned heavily on EDM, Rave and Rap moved in. However, Jet and his mates remained steadfast in their allegiance to mainstream rock, heavily influenced by icons like Foghat, Savoy Brown, and Queen.

Jet, now sixteen-years-old, was fully immersed in music and girls. He formed the band Fractured Butterfly. To him, the name was a symbol of transformation, of breaking free from the constraints of society and embracing individuality. But deep down, the name held a deeper meaning, a subconscious tribute to Lily, and the fractured pieces of her innocence that she had lost at such a tender age.

Jet and Lily shared an unspoken bond. His protective instincts kicked in whenever Lily was around, evidenced by the silent language of shared glances and comforting touches that spoke volumes without the need for words. Despite the six-year age gap, Jet always saw Lily as more than just a family acquaintance; she had become his confidante and closest friend, despite the distance between them. Over the past few years, their bond only grew stronger as they exchanged letters and had long-distance phone conversations when her grandparents were calling abroad to friends and family.

Lily was back for a summer visit and, as with most weekends, the band would practice for hours in an abandoned garage down the street from where he lived. Jet was an only child to older parents who indulged his creative outlets. He wrote his first song at ten, and they bought him his own guitar after his father taught him a few chords on his.

The band had never played gigs for money, but practiced like they did. Kids from all around the neighborhood would show up to watch them play and hang out. When Lily was in town, she loved to watch them and thought they were actually pretty good.

She would sit on the boot of Jet's father's car, and between songs, he would come over and check on her. Some of the other boys in the band had girlfriends, and they would sit with her and keep her company. She dreamed of being one of them, watching the boy she loved singing in a rock and roll band.

As the band wrapped up a Saturday morning rehearsal, Lily noticed a bouncy little red-headed Irish girl approach the car where everyone was congregating around her. The new girl, along with the others, were buzzing with anticipation, and were eager to kick off their weekend plans. Lily spoke up and asked what they were going to do. The new girl said, "Me Da is taking us to the Cavern Club tonight. We're all leaving after rehearsal and den spending de night at our holiday home. We'll be back Sunday night!"

"Wow!" Lily said, "That sounds like fun!"

Jet strolled over to the car, but today there was a shift in his focus. Without so much as a glance in her direction, he reached for the new girl, pulling her close around the waist, and kissed her. Right on the mouth!!

Finally, he turned his attention to her. "Lily, this is Gemma. Did they tell you about tonight?" He positioned himself behind the girl, continuing to hold her.

Lily sat frozen, her heart sinking as disbelief clouded her vision. She couldn't believe the betrayal. She responded with a barely audible, "Yep." While the rest of the group voiced their excitement about their upcoming adventure, Lily remained shocked with an aching realization. She had never seen Jet display affection towards anyone in such a manner. A whirlwind of questions tormented her. What did this mean? Did he not love her anymore? The longer she watched them, the more irritated she got.

Jet, bubbling with excitement, held his hand out to help Lily get off the car and said, "C'mon Lily, we need to get home; I need to finish getting packed."

Green-eyed, Lily slid off the boot, accepting his help, and swiftly gripped Jet's wrist, pulling him away from Gemma in a determined display of possession. Jet turned back to Gemma with a shrug and said, "I guess I'll see you in a bit?" She nodded and gave him a little wave as he turned back to Lily. "What's your hurry? I still gotta get my gear!"

Lily stopped pulling him, looked up, and snarked, "I thought you needed to pack?"

"I do, I'll be right back," he said, a hint of irritation darkening his voice as he gently pried Lily's fingers from his wrist before returning to his mates. They had already packed up, so he shouldered his guitar case and grabbed the rest of his equipment and returned to the car.

Lily, having climbed into the car, turned on her knees to glare at the girls from over the passenger seat as he filled the boot. He closed the lid, and she watched as he kissed Gemma one last time before getting into the car.

The girls, feeling the weight of Lily's death glare, watched uneasily as Jet slid into the car beside her.

"What was all that about?" Gemma asked, her expression a mix of discomfort and curiosity.

One of the girlfriends, Penny, who was the friendliest to Lily, laughed out loud. "I almost feel bad for you," the girls looked at her. "Oh, don't you know? They're basically attached at the hip." Penny walked away to meet up with Ronny, shaking her head, then turned back as she reached him, saying, "Good luck ."

Gemma stood confused, watching as Jet drove off.

Jet attempted to break the silence in the car as they drove back home. "Lily?" His voice carried a hint of uncertainty.

She remained silent, refusing to acknowledge him.

"Lily?" he tried again, his tone a touch louder this time, tinged with concern. "Are you mad at me or something?"

A pang of guilt struck him at Lily's curt response. "Or something," she huffed, arms crossed defiantly as she gazed out the window.

Sighing softly, Jet decided not to press the matter further. He understood Lily well enough to recognize when it was best to let her simmer down on her own. Remembering past instances of her anger directed toward others, he silently thanked his stars that she had never directed that fury toward him. Yet.

The rest of the ride home was silent. Thank goodness it was a short one. When they pulled up to the house, Lily got out and started walking down the street. "Hey! Where are you going?" Jet's heart raced as Lily ignored his call, her determined stride down the street unwavering. Panic surged within him, knowing she was still too young and unfamiliar with the area to be walking alone. He leaped out of the car and chased after her.

Determined not to let her slip away, Jet caught up to her, his arms encircling her waist as he lifted her off the ground. For a moment, he twirled her around, hoping to break through the wall of silence that had fallen between them. Usually, she loved being twirled by him. But not today! With Lily still cradled in his arms, he started walking back to the house, holding her in front of him.

"Put me down!" she yelled.

"C'mon, Lily girl, you can't be mad at me. What did I do?"

"Now!"

He stopped and set her on her feet.

She stomped off. "I want to go home."

"Okay ... I'll take you home."

"NO! I want Pops to take me home."

"Okay! Okay, I'll get Pops to drive you home."

Confused by her outburst, he followed her into the house. Lily stormed into the kitchen where Mum was and plopped into a chair at the table. Jet found his father and told him Lily wanted 'POPS' to take her home. That was her name for Jet's father.

During their visits to the UK, Lily divided her time almost equally between her great-uncle's and Jet's home. Her grandfather would jest that she was like community property, a notion that brought a smile to Lily's face. Jet's parents welcomed her into their family with open arms, treating her as if she were their own. Gradually, Lily grew so comfortable with them she began calling them Mum and Pops, just like Jet did.

"You can't take her home?" Pops questioned, looking up from his chair.

"She doesn't want me to take her; she's mad at me?"

"What did you do?"

"I don't know," Jet complained, his frustration clear. "She was fine during rehearsal, and after I introduced her to Gemma and mentioned this weekend's plans, she got all weird and wouldn't even talk to me. She's never acted like that before. And then, when we got here, she just jumped out of the car and started walking down the street. I ran after her, and she yelled at me, saying she wanted to go home. I offered to take her, but she said no, she wanted you!"

"Ohhh..." Pops nodded, understanding the situation. "I see."

"What?"

Pops shook his head and stood. "Let me get the keys."

"What?!"

Pops sighed, "Son, did you talk to Lily about Gemma before introducing her."

"No, why?"

"You really don't know?"

"Know what? I wish someone would tell me what's going on!"

"Son, you know Lily loves you, right?"

"I know. I love her too."

"No, son, Lily is *in* love with you. She always has been."

"What? No, she's like ... my little sister."

"That's not how she sees it."

Jet sat down on the couch. "She's way too little for me."

"I know that, and you know that..." He looked Jet square in the face. "You better know that."

Jet looked snidely at his father. "Of course I know!"

"She, however, does not know that. What she does know is that you make her feel safe. You two spend a considerable amount of time together. You dote on her when she's here. You eat most of your meals together, and you take her everywhere. The two of you talk for hours, both here and on the phone—Lord knows we've spent a mint on those long-distance conversations!"

"Geez, you make us sound like you and Mum."

Pops raised his eyebrows at Jet. "Exactly."

Realizing his father's point, Jet put his head in his hands. "Oh man ... what do I do?"

"Well," he said, shrugging. "Either she'll grow out of it, or we'll start planning a wedding." He laughed, putting the keys in his pocket and throwing on a sweater.

Jet looked up at his father. "You're not helping." He got up and started walking toward his room.

"Seriously, though," Jet turned to listen. "Son, now that you have a steady girlfriend, she knows this girl is going to take up a lot of your time. She's jealous, and rightly so. You should have told her about Gemma before introducing them and explained things. I can't believe that you haven't figured this out yet. Lily has always been vocal about her feelings for you. She hasn't hidden anything."

"I just thought she was playing. You know, how little girls play house."

"Have you ever known Lily to play like other little girls? John, she isn't just any little girl. She doesn't even talk like a little girl. I've heard some of the conversations you have with her. Listening to her talk, you'd think she's lived an entire lifetime. She's smart, John. She sees the world a little differently than you and I. She's had to grow up pretty fast with what she's gone through."

"I know, but it's different with her. We just talk. About all kinds of stuff. I don't talk to her like I talk to girls."

"And she knows that. Why do you think she's so upset? She knows you better than any of these girls you bring home. Son, *you* need to remember that whether you see it or not, she is a real girl with real girl feelings."

"It's hard to think of her like that when she still crawls onto my lap and falls asleep watching Top of the Pops, and when we're at the park playing football, she's like ... just one of us."

"Yes, of course, she is, and it's perfectly normal for you to feel this way. I just thought you understood how *she* felt. It may be time to try to distance yourself from her a little. Maybe introduce her to people her own age. Don't any of your friends have younger siblings?"

"I guess?" He shrugged.

"Something to think about."

"Yeah, maybe I could find her some new friends here."

Pops patted him on the shoulder on their way out of the room. "I'm sure you two will figure it out, eventually."

"I hope so."

The house had thin walls, so Lily and Mum overheard Jet and Pop's conversation. Mum was drying dishes, the clinking of plates and cups filled the air, creating a backdrop to the hushed tones of the conversation. They remained silent, listening. Mum watched for her reactions but felt Lily needed to hear it.

As the conversation ended, Lily turned to Mum with tear-filled eyes, absorbing the weight of Pop's words. Mum completed her task of putting the last dish away, draping the towel over her shoulder before settling down in front of Lily. Taking her hand gently, Mum spoke with a tone of reassurance. "Lily, honey, you know we all love you, right?" Lily nodded silently, her eyes fixed on Mum's face. "We just think you should try to enjoy being a little girl while you can. One of these days, you'll be an old married lady like me and wish you had spent more of your childhood having fun."

Lily nodded as she dropped her head, tears dripping into her lap. Pops entered the room and found her. He immediately sensed her distress. Without a word, he gave Mum a reassuring glance, then guided Lily gently to the car, understanding that she may need some time away from the house.

Starting the engine, Pops drove towards her great-uncle's place, allowing Lily to process her thoughts and emotions in peace. After a few moments of silence, Pops spoke, hoping he could explain things to her.

"Lily?"

"Yeah, Pops?"

"I hear you're angry with Jet?"

She looked out of the window and answered, "No ... not anymore... just sad."

"Why sad?"

"Because I'm only ten ... but I'll be eleven in a week."

"Honey, you know John's older than you, and he's going to have girlfriends, right?"

She sighed. "I know, but I'm not going to have any boyfriends," she said matter-of-factly.

"Oh, I think if the right boy came along, you might change your mind."

"But he has come along, Pops. He just doesn't know it yet ... but I can wait." Pops glanced at Lily, his heart aching for the innocence mingled with the complexity of her emotions. Then she added, "You know, when I'm twenty, Jet will only be twenty-six. He won't be too old for me then, will he?"

"No, doll, I guess you're right. He won't be too old for you then."

"See, it'll work out." She nodded, trying to convince herself, and looked back out the window. Pops gave her a weak smile and patted her on her knee, realizing his efforts were futile.

Chapter Ten

All Aboard

(2002)

With the chores done for the day and dinner cleared, Levi sank into the plush cushions of his recliner in front of the television. Meanwhile, Daria stepped out onto the front deck and sat in the rocking chair to enjoy the sunset. The sky, ablaze with vibrant hues of orange and pink, drew her to her favorite spot. Luckily, the cabin faced westward, offering Daria an unobstructed view from their little valley homestead. She came out tonight to get some distance from Levi and strategize her next move. They were being watched somehow, so she would need to devise a better plan, one that would evade any prying eyes.

In recent months, Daria found life with Levi increasingly challenging. She didn't think he was cut out for life in a domestic-type scenario. Sure, Levi excelled in the day-to-day demands of farm life but cohabitation with another human—not so much.

Levi grappled with his role in their shared situation. It was clear, and whether he realized it or not, he had traded one prison life for another. She was sure that what he had mistaken for freedom had only trapped him, and he was getting restless.

Levi's drinking had spiraled, reaching a point where he began his mornings with beer and ended his days with liquor. Daria watched helplessly as his behavior grew more and more erratic, especially since

Uncle's weekly visits had stopped. She thought out of sight, out of mind, and fear of their warden since Uncle only made monthly appearances now with the doctor. Without Uncle's protective presence, she found herself vulnerable, left to navigate the storm of Levi's behavior on her own.

As the sun disappeared over the horizon, the temperature dropped, and Daria decided it was time to head inside. As she made her way in, Daria couldn't shake the feeling of dread that gnawed at her insides. Levi was still awake, likely nursing another drink in the dimly lit living room, but she took her chances and tried to head straight to her room.

Upon entering through the door, Daria's heart sank at the sight of Levi stumbling clumsily towards her from the kitchen, a half-empty bottle of liquor clutched tightly in his grasp.

Before she could react, Levi lurched forward and grabbed her, his grip tightening around her in a drunken embrace. His words dripped with venomous intent as he spoke, his breath hot against her skin. "Hey, Girl," he slurred, his voice thick with intoxication, "how about ya let me treat ya like a proper wife tonight?"

"Levi, go lay down, you're drunk." She struggled to get out of his grasp.

He squeezed her tighter. "C'mon, now ... I'll be real good to ya."

"Levi, you're hurting me. Now stop it!" Still trying to push away from him.

The air crackled with tension as Levi's frustration boiled over, his voice rising to a growl. "Woman," he spat, his words slurred, "you're gonna treat me like a proper husband even if I have to make you!"

As they stumbled backward towards Levi's bedroom, Daria got one hand loose from his grip and slapped him across the face as hard as she could.

The force of the blow sent shockwaves as Levi dropped the bottle and stumbled back a step and let go of her. "You bitch!" His eyes flashed with rage as he lunged forward and, with a guttural growl, he pinned her hands against the wall on either side of her head, his knee crushing between her legs, immobilizing her with his sheer dominance.

"I told ya before, I like it the hard way." Then he buried his head into her neck, licking her. "Ya taste real good, girl..." he groaned. "Ya know, I could take you right where you stand."

"Levi, please! I'm gonna tell Uncle." It was the only real threat she thought he would fear. "He told you not to touch me until after the baby was born."

He pushed himself back, leaving only an inch or two between them, and delivered a furious punch to the wall beside her face. The impact echoed through the room, the force of it causing the plaster to crack and crumble under his assault.

Staggering backward, Levi's movements were unsteady as he slurred, "Fuck you!" With one final cutting glare at Daria, he turned and stumbled out of the house, leaving her shaken in the wake of his violent outburst.

She didn't know where he was going, and at that point, she didn't care. A quick glance at the key rack told her he wasn't going far, and because he would pull the EFI fuse when he got out of the truck every time he drove it, neither was she. So, Daria locked herself in her bedroom that night and every night after, finding safety in the thin barrier of the door.

The next morning, she stumbled upon him unconscious in the barn. She left him to wake on his own, thinking it was better to stay away from him as much as possible.

Last night's episode with Levi only made her more determined to return to Jet. She had to be smart about it this time. She was getting too big for an escape on foot, but it had to happen sooner than later.

Several days later, while on their weekly trip to town, they stumbled upon a new grocery store with a built-in pharmacy. It was a stroke of luck that the store caught their attention, and they explored it despite being further away from their usual route.

Levi thought it would be worth the extra distance if it could save him an additional trip to the pharmacy.

Daria noticed the grocery store at this location had a bus station a few doors down. On most occasions, Levi usually stayed in the truck, dozing, only coming in when he needed more beer or if he wanted something in particular. But on this trip, he followed her in to check the layout and see if anything caught his eye.

After several more excursions, Levi's interest waned, and so on this last trip, as Levi dozed in the truck, she snuck out the back of the store and ran down to the station to get a bus schedule, testing how long it would take her to get there.

Daria had been skimming the extra change from the grocery money, stashing it away little by little. She was biding her time until she had enough for a bus ticket, a tangible step towards her freedom.

A few evenings later, during one of her routine checkups, the doctor arrived without Uncle. The Brit accompanied her instead. While always impeccably dressed, the Brit gave off an unsettling vibe that Daria couldn't shake off. He lacked a top hat, but his beady, sunken eyes, stringy, unkempt hair, and a high-pitched lull when he spoke to her evoked the eerie image of the creepy child catcher from the movie Chitty Chitty Bang Bang, sending shivers down her spine.

"Where's Uncle?" Daria asked.

"Oh, he's gone away on business, Deary," the Brit said.

"Away, where?"

"On the other side of the pond, I'm afraid."

The doctor gave him a warning look and then called him by name, "Giles!"

"Oh, but he'll be back real soon. Don't you worry."

"Are you ready for your checkup?" the doctor asked, redirecting the conversation.

Daria nodded and headed into the bedroom. While the doctor looked her over, she spotted a couple of fading bruises. "What's this?" She held Daria's wrist up to examine it.

"Oh, it's nothing. Just an accident while I was working around the barn," she said, hoping to deflect further inquiry, still not trusting the doctor's motives. The doctor didn't believe her, but she didn't question her further. "You must be careful now. An injury could harm not only you but the baby too."

"Yes ... I'll be more careful."

After the appointment, the doctor and Giles left, reiterating that Uncle would return soon. Daria stayed in her room. The soft glow of the evening sun filtered through the curtains, casting a warm hue over the space. She sank onto the edge of her bed, the warm quilt beneath her providing a sense of comfort. With a sigh of relief, she reached under the mattress and retrieved her hidden stash. "I should have enough to get me away from here," she murmured to herself, a glimmer of hope igniting within her. The plan was set, and she was ready to reclaim her freedom.

Just then, the baby gave her a sturdy kick. "Whoa there..." She rubbed her belly. "We're gonna be okay ... just as soon as I get us out of here." She sighed.

The next morning, she asked Levi to take her to the store.

"It ain't our day yet."

"I know, but I have a prescription, and you just drank your last beer. Plus, the baby will be here soon, and I need to stock up on a few items."

"Ah hell, girl." He grabbed the keys. "Let's go. Get in the truck."

"Are you okay to drive?"

"Hell yeah," he slurred. She was glad he was already feeling the effects of his liquid breakfast, because it would guarantee her time to make her escape while he dozed.

When they got there, he told her he wasn't going in. *Thank God!* He then told her to grab his beer for him.

She nodded and headed in. She grabbed a basket, stood out of sight, and watched until he dozed off. As soon as she thought he was out, she headed for the back door.

At the bus station, she asked for the first and furthest ticket she had enough money for.

"You in a hurry, honey?" the older lady behind the counter inquired.

"Yes, ma'am."

"Well, I think I can get you as far as Atlanta, Hun."

"When does it leave?"

"In about thirty minutes. See there." The woman pointed to the front of the building.

"They're loading her up right now."

"I'll take it."

"Here ya go." She handed her the ticket. "They'll call for y'all in a few minutes. You can sit over there while you wait."

Daria took the ticket with a nod of thanks, her heart racing with the prospect of escape. Finding a seat, she settled in, clutching her ticket tightly in her hand and scanning the area. This was it—the first tangible step in a long while towards a life she hoped to reclaim.

Daria stood up, taking a deep breath as the call for her bus was announced. Finding her seat on the bus, Daria settled in, the worn fabric of the seat brushed rough against her skin in the warm afternoon sun.

As the bus rumbled to life and moved, Daria caught a fleeting glimpse of the truck with Levi still napping inside, oblivious to her departure. Her mind wandered to the task of finding a safe place to reach out to her family once she reached Atlanta.

Outside, the landscape blurred into a green mosaic, punctuated by the occasional farmhouse or stand of trees. She sank deeper into her seat, the soft murmur of conversations blending with the rhythmic hum of the bus engine.

The warmth of the sun filtering through the window and the gentle vibration of the bus created a calming atmosphere that coaxed her into a state of contemplation. Her hand instinctively rested on her belly as she drifted in and out of reverie, carried by the rhythm of the journey.

Chapter Eleven

Lessons in Futility

(1997)

The summer Lily turned thirteen marked not only the shift into her teenage years but also the loss of her beloved grandmother, Gillie. For Lily, her grandmother had been more than that. She was a guiding light, a confidante, and the closest semblance of a mother figure in her life.

The loss shattered her grandfather as well. The grief that washed over him was deep and, in the weeks following Gillie's passing, given that Wallace was now retired, the family collectively decided that Lily and Wallace should move to England to live with Abe and Minnie. Abe, a man of warmth and stability, and Minnie, with her nurturing presence, offered a new beginning and a promise of continuity in the face of their profound loss. The move to England not only provided comfort for Wallace, but it also ushered in a new chapter for Lily.

In the tranquil English countryside of a nearby village, Lily could finally go to a proper school. Here, amidst the rolling green hills and quaint cobblestone streets, she could find a reprieve from the relentless turmoil caused by Rob's presence back in the States. The ivy-covered walls of the village school beckoned. As she stepped through the threshold of the school gates, a sense of belonging washed over her, filling the void left by years of uncertainty.

Meanwhile, over the past year, Jet's band, Fractured Butterfly, had been making waves in the local music scene, enabling him to move out of his parents' home and into a flat of sorts with the other boys from the band.

They found an old petrol station in a small village, about twenty minutes away, that had gone out of business, so they contacted the landowner and offered to rent it.

Transforming the old station into a rehearsal and living space was a project driven by both necessity and creativity. With the pumps removed, the overhang, once a shelter for customers pumping petrol, now provided the perfect canopy for the van that carried their most precious cargo—their instruments.

They brought in old couches and rugs, transforming the once cold, hard space into a warm and comfortable haven. Posters and lights adorned the walls, reflecting their tastes and influences, turning the garage into a sanctuary of artistic expression.

There were three large separate rooms and a bathroom upstairs that had been an office and storage area. The boys, along with some help from their parents and girlfriends, cleaned the place out and made them into sleeping quarters.

Jet and the other band members worked various jobs during the week and played shows on the weekends, which didn't leave Jet much time for Lily.

She was able to go to some of the more local gigs the boys played if they were in parks or family-friendly pubs, but they were few and far between.

Since most of the shows took place out of town, and he spent his weekends traveling, they kept in touch much the same way they did when she lived in the States—by phone. Only now, there were no long-distance charges, as long as they were in the same exchange area, so they could at least talk more.

In the cozy, makeshift world the boys had created within the old garage, after dinner and homework, evenings unwound with Lily and Jet discussing his hatred for his boss and his hopes of hitting it big and being able to quit. Lily had no complaints as school was a haven for her, a place of learning and growth she secretly cherished.

Much to the chagrin of her family and his bandmates, together they would often find themselves lost in the world of television, each on one end of the line, watching in silence, only breaking it to share a thought or laugh during the breaks.

Late one evening, the ringing of the phone shattered the quiet of the Lovell home. It was Jet. Minnie came down to answer the phone and chastised him for calling so late. She told him to call back in the morning, that Lily was already asleep, but Lily heard the ring too and rushed down. "Who is it, Auntie?"

"It's Jet. He knows better than to call this late."

Lily finished running down the stairs and grabbed the phone out of her aunt's hands. "Jet!"

Her aunt Shhh'd her and pointed that she was going back upstairs. "Don't stay on the phone too long, young lady; it's a school night."

Lily nodded as she passed, then rolled her eyes and whispered into the phone. "Hey, are you okay?"

"Yeah, I just needed to hear a friendly voice." His tone was heavy with unspoken burdens.

Lily slid down the wall to sit. "You found one." He half laughed.

She heard him take a long breath. "Is everything okay? What's the matter?" She prodded gently.

"I don't really want to talk about it." It was Lily's turn to half laugh.

"But you called?" she said, a little confused.

"I don't want to talk about it ... with you," he corrected, his words landing heavy.

Her heart ached at his admission, but she swallowed the sting. "Okay..." She detected a little bit of a slur in his voice and wondered if he'd been drinking.

"May I ask why?"

"It's complicated ... you wouldn't understand..." He laughed again. "Who am I kidding? You're probably the only one who would understand."

"All you have to do is talk, Jet ... whether I understand or not, I can still listen."

His response lingered in the air, a reluctant acknowledgment of the complications of the bond between them. "That's why I love you, Lily girl—you always put up with my crap, even when you shouldn't have to."

Her heart cried when he spoke those words. Every time. Those words didn't mean to him what they meant to her, but still, he loved her and that was all she needed—for now.

"I love you too," she whispered hoarsely, her heart breaking with every syllable.

Silence stretched for a long moment, Jet's unspoken emotions circling before his voice broke. "I'm sorry, Lil."

Before she could respond, the line went dead. Speechless, she put the receiver back in its cradle. Tears streamed down her face as she held the phone in her lap. Her aunt, who had been listening at the top of the stairs, started down to check on her.

When she reached the bottom step, Lily got up and handed her the phone. "Oh, Lily, what's happened, love?"

Wiping her face dry, Lily shrugged. "He wouldn't tell me."

After giving her aunt a quick kiss goodnight on the cheek, she began climbing the stairs.

Her aunt stood holding the phone, watching Lily trod slowly up each step, shaking her head and grumbling under her breath, "Men."

Lily hadn't heard from Jet for several days. Worried, on the third day of no contact, a sense of unease forced her into action. She dressed in her school uniform and headed out as usual. Skipping classes, she made her way to his place, arriving before him, and sat out front to meet him.

Ronny, the bass player, was the first to arrive. He was tall and slim, but athletic. He had been on track to become a football player, but an injury forced him to quit. His hair was light blonde and long, almost mid-back, and permed into spirals. His fair complexion contrasted well with the black leather pants and concert tees he always wore. From the beginning, Ronny always looked like a rock star.

He greeted her with a big smile that met his round blue eyes, and said, "Ello, love, what brings you to our humble abode?"

"I'm worried about Jet," she said. "I haven't heard from him. He called the other night, upset about something ... he wouldn't tell me what."

"Ah," he answered as he unlocked the main door. Lily got up and followed him.

"Ah, what?"

"Listen, Lovey, I don't feel comfortable telling you his business, but suffice it to say, he has been on a tear lately."

"I got that much, Ronny, but what's really going on?"

He opened the door and invited her in. She came in, put her bag down, and watched as he opened the garage doors to let in fresh air. As he took his time returning, she sat on a stool at their makeshift kitchen bar, waiting to finish their conversation. It was apparent to her that he was uncomfortable and didn't want to discuss it.

"Ronny?" Adding steel to her tone this time. "Tell me what's going on?"

"Honestly, I don't know. Some nights, he comes home. Some nights, he doesn't. I figure he's off with some young bint, but who knows? And on the nights he is here, he's been absolutely badgered. He doesn't talk about it much."

"Where is Lorna?" she asked, curious about his current girlfriend.

"That was over ages ago. She said she didn't like the club scene, but Penny thinks she didn't enjoy jockeying for his attention with you." Lily's brows furrowed at this revelation, her mind swirling with thoughts. "He's more into one-nighters these days." Ronny sensed her concern and moved to sit beside her, offering a comforting touch to her knee. "I think he's frustrated, Lily. We haven't found a manager he trusts, and he wants to self-produce an EP, but some of the other guys aren't as serious as he is about making this an actual career. They're just having a bit of a laugh. It's all fun and games for them." He shrugged, a gesture tinged with resignation.

"What about you?"

"Oh, I'm all in. I don't want to work in a factory for the rest of my life. Penny and I need this, and Jet does, too."

She pursed her lips in understanding and nodded. "Okay, so let's do something about it."

"Like what?"

"Well," Lily contemplated, rising to her feet and placing her hands on her hips, a determined glimmer in her eye. "To start, what about having a band meeting to find out who's serious and who isn't? Boot anyone not interested and hold auditions to replace them. Then, start setting goals." Her voice held a note of firmness, signaling her readiness to take charge of the situation.

Surprised, Ronny leaned back in his chair, crossed his arms, and stared at her. "I'm listening."

Pacing back and forth in front of him, Lily continued, her words measured and confident. "If you're really serious about making it, you can't rely on getting discovered. Not here anyway ... and you'll need to play bigger venues. I know you can sell the tickets. I've heard you play; they love you." Her conviction echoed in the room, underlining her belief in their potential.

She walked over to where the band equipment was set up for rehearsals and then turned around to look at him. "And you need to look like a band. Hair, make-up, clothes, and whatever else makes you stand out," she asserted, emphasizing the importance of not just sounding like a cohesive group but also presenting a memorable image on stage.

She strolled around the setup, studying the instruments, then ran her finger down the neck of Jet's guitar. "Jet's right, you know ... about producing your own EP." She paused, still concentrating on the rig setup, then fired off a barrage of questions. "Ronny? How much does it cost to live here? Can you live here on your salary, or do you need the gig money, too? Do you think the guys would be willing to pool your gig money?" She stopped and turned to face him. "If you could pool your gig money, you could afford some studio time. Then we could take a demo to the radio stations. Or ... we could even make copies and sell them at your shows. We could have all our friends and fans call the radio stations and request your songs. It could spark their curiosity, and maybe, if they play it, you could find a manager.

What do you think?" She shrugged, her hands open for commentary, awaiting Ronny's response.

Speechless, Ronny sat there until they both noticed Jet leaning on the open garage door, listening. "I think we found our new manager," he said, smiling as he approached.

She ran to him and hugged him around his waist. He greeted her with a kiss on top of her head before turning to Ronny. "So, what do you think?"

Ronny put his arms out in acceptance and said, "It sounds like a plan."

"Wait, what part? Me being the manager or just the plan?" Lily asked, a playful grin on her face.

"Both!" they declared in unison, sharing a smile at her enthusiasm.

"But seriously, Lil, I'm not too sure how keen our mates will be about a thirteen-year-old manager." He squeezed her a little tighter before letting her go.

"Almost fourteen," she corrected. "Plus, I'm free ... and besides, they don't have to know. You'll be the manager. I'll just be your secretary. You guys need a lot of help, and I have the time to do it."

"Honestly, I don't know why we didn't think of some of this ourselves," Ronny said, scratching his head.

"I know why." Both boys looked at her. "Three reasons: girls, booze, and because you're the talent. What you need is brains. That's where I come in." She nodded confidently, crossing her arms.

They looked back at each other and smiled again, not taking her seriously.

"I'm serious! I can make phone calls to recruit friends and fans. The girls and I could help with the wardrobe, and we could even run a booth for sales at your shows.... C'mooon, let me help!" She flounced.

"Okay, Okay!"

"Yay!" she squealed, jumping up and clapping. Then she stopped dead in her tracks. "Okay, there's so much to do! I gotta go!" She rushed over to grab her bag and headed out the garage door.

Both boys stood silent, watching as she got past the door, stopped, turned around, and headed back in. "So, what are you guys, anyway? Rock ... Glam ... Punk?"

Both boys declared, "Rock!" She turned and headed out again.

Then stopped, turned around, and walked back into the garage, dropping her bag on the ground beside her in defeat. "I need a ride home. I spent all my money coming here." She frowned. They laughed. "C'mon, Lily girl, I promised Mum I would stop by this week, anyway." Jet pulled the van keys from his pocket and headed out with her.

(2002)

As the bus came to a halt at the station in Atlanta, Daria stirred from her slumber, her heart pounding with excitement. With a rush of adrenaline, she grabbed her bag and rose from her seat, eager to step off the bus and into freedom. Casting a cautious glance through the windows as fellow passengers walked by, she scanned the surroundings, searching for any signs of police or payphones. If she could locate an officer, she could share her harrowing tale and enlist their help in finding her way home. After enduring months of captivity, the prospect of liberation filled her with hope and determination. At long last, her moment of freedom had arrived.

Then she spotted them. Daria's heart sank as she was walking down the aisle. They were standing with a police officer, pointing at the bus, showing him a picture. *No, no, no.* Silent screams echoed in her mind, her worst nightmare unfolding before her eyes.

Feeling the weight of uncertainty, Daria sank into the nearest seat, unsure whether to take her chances and run after getting off the bus or try to convince the officer of her plight. She held her belly and thought better of running.

When the bus emptied, the police officer boarded, took a second look at the picture, and asked if this was her. She closed her eyes, refusing to answer. "It seems you have some concerned people looking for you." He pointed out the window and asked, "Do you know those people?"

Daria shook her head. "I don't know them! They took me away from my family. I'm just trying to get home."

"Yeah, they said you'd say something like that."

"It's true; they've held me for months at a farm in Kentucky, and I was able to get away. Please ... help me," she begged him.

"Listen, my dispatch checked their credentials while we were waiting on your bus, and everything checked out. They have paperwork proving guardianship, and you're still a minor. They're saying that you ran away from a girl's home where your parents sent you to have your baby. I even had them call the home. It, too, is legit. So, I'm afraid I have to believe them." "They're lying. I'm not a minor. I'm eighteen; I can prove it." She opened her bag and pulled out a small pad of paper. "These are the numbers of my family and my boyfriend ... Please!" she pleaded. "Call them. They'll tell you who I am. I swear!" Desperation tinged her words as she clung to the hope that her loved ones could vouch for her true identity.

He got on his walkie and gave the numbers to the person on the other end. After a minute, the person asked, "Where are these located?"

"England." Daria's heart raced as she watched the officer relay her plea. The voice on the radio said they would have to get approval to call another country. The officer sat down in the seat across from her to wait. Daria, again, pleaded with him to believe her and detailed her story.

Daria's stomach churned as she locked eyes with the doctor and Giles. His ominous grin sent a shiver through her, casting doubt on her chances of escaping their clutches once more.

A few minutes later, the voice on the walkie returned and said that all the numbers had been disconnected or were not in service. Daria screeched, "NOOO, that can't be. Not all of them!" The despair in her voice echoed at the realization that her lifelines to the outside world seemed to have vanished.

"I'd like to believe you. You seem like a nice enough girl, but nothing you have told me can be corroborated. I'm sorry. I'm going to have to let them take you back."

"Noooo!" she sobbed.

The police officer exited the bus, spoke to the two briefly, and then looked back at Daria. She could see that he had doubts, but his hands were tied. He waited outside the bus while the two boarded.

Daria screamed, "I'm not going back! You can't make me!"

Giles grabbed her by the arm, and Daria began fighting with him. She laid back in the seat, slapping and kicking, not allowing him to get a grip on her.

Seeing the commotion, the police officer got back on the bus. "Is that necessary?"

The doctor told him she would have to sedate Daria, so she wouldn't hurt the baby and asked for a wheelchair. He called for his partner to bring one and helped Giles hold her down while the doctor stabbed the needle in her leg. It only took seconds for Daria to go limp.

Again, she woke back in her bed in Kentucky. The cycle of captivity continued, leaving her trapped in a nightmarish loop with no clear escape.

Chapter Twelve

Jack

(2003)

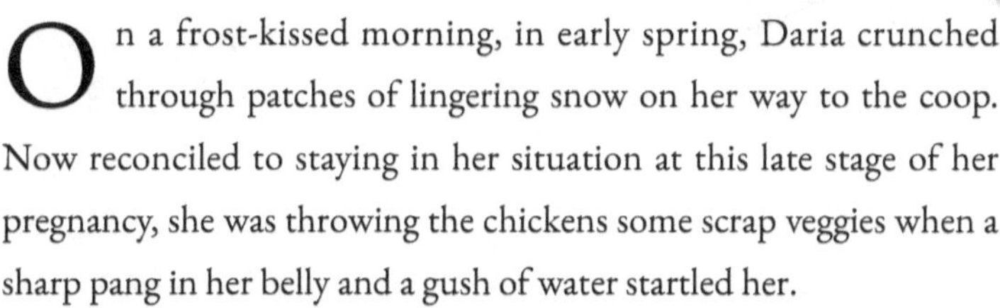

On a frost-kissed morning, in early spring, Daria crunched through patches of lingering snow on her way to the coop. Now reconciled to staying in her situation at this late stage of her pregnancy, she was throwing the chickens some scrap veggies when a sharp pang in her belly and a gush of water startled her.

She gasped, her hand instinctively clutching her belly. Her emotions swirled with a turbulent mix of nervousness, excitement, fear, and maybe some hint of relief. "LEVI!" she shouted.

He came around the corner, concerned after hearing the tone of her voice. She looked over at him. "My water broke."

"Well, shit. I thought we had another couple of weeks?"

"I don't think anyone informed the baby."

"C'mon girl, let's get you inside. I gotta run down and call the doctor." He helped her to the front door.

"I've got it from here."

Levi took off in the truck while Daria went in and cleaned up. She figured it would probably take hours before anything significant happened, so she showered off, put on an old nightgown, and sat on the edge of the bed.

Sooner than expected, she felt stronger twinges and her belly tightening. *A little more uncomfortable, but bearable.* She thought as she breathed through them.

Levi returned to find her in the bedroom, lying on her side. He informed her, "Doc said she was on the way, and there should be plenty of time." Daria nodded and continued to breathe through the tougher ones.

Levi opened the refrigerator, popped open a beer, and then paced the living room, looking out the window every so often, waiting for the doctor. He finished that beer in record time and popped open another. By the time he opened the third beer, Daria's contractions had rapidly increased in strength. He could hear her panting. He walked into the bedroom.

She saw him and cried, "I don't think they're going to make it."

"What!?"

"I think it's coming ... NOW!" she groaned in fear and agony, "Levi ... you have to ... catch the baby!" she cried out, panting through another contraction.

"I don't know nothin' bout birthin' no baby!" he snapped back.

"You helped ... Daisy!"

"She's a cow!"

"It all works the same, Levi!"

"OH Hell!" He ran to the bathroom, washed his hands, and grabbed some clean towels. When he returned, he pulled the covers off her and helped her turn sideways on the bed.

He got down on his knees and positioned himself on the floor below her. Levi lifted her gown up over her knees and smirked, "This ain't exactly how I pictured myself gettin' inta yer britches."

"SHUT ... UP!" she wailed. "AHHHH ... It's coming!"

"I see it! Keep Pushing!"

Clutching her knees tightly, she breathed a final groan and used all the rest of her strength, pushing with every fiber of her being. It was as if her entire body was being twisted inside out as this tiny life tore its way through her. Then, finally, relief washed over her.

She laid back, panting and crying. She was exhausted and relieved that her baby was finally here and mourning the fact Jet was not. Again, wondering if he would ever meet his child.

Levi had the baby in his hands and announced it was a boy as the doctor and Uncle scrambled into the room.

The doctor rushed to take the baby from his hands. She wrapped him in a towel and laid him on Daria's chest so she could finish the process. Uncle stood beside the bed for a moment, overseeing the doctor's work.

"Very good." He nodded and then inspected the child.

"A boy, you said?" He looked back at Levi standing by the bedroom door.

"Yeah," he answered, then turned and went to the bathroom to wash. When he finished, he walked to the kitchen, grabbed a beer, and popped it open. He stood there staring at the closed refrigerator door. *Well, shit! Here we go ...* then took a long gulp and went and sat in his recliner.

Uncle finished his inspection and walked outside to wait for the doctor. She finished with Daria and gave instructions for her self-care. "You will need time to heal. I will be back tomorrow. Levi will call if there are any complications, yes?" Daria nodded as she cooed and held her tiny son. "Do you have a name?"

"Jack. It's short for John, his father's name."

"Do you think this is a wise choice? It would be a constant reminder of his father. The child has a new father now. You said you would try to make this work. You agreed that no more attempts would be made to escape."

Daria glared at her, then fumed, "First, I never said I would try to make this work! And as far as a reminder? Just looking into this beautiful boy's eyes every day will be a constant reminder of what we have lost. Levi may have agreed to his deal. He knew what he was getting himself into. I didn't agree to anything. I was forced, and while I have no choice but to stay, I will never learn to like it here. I will never love him as a husband, nor will I ever forget Jet and my family in England." The raw emotion and resentment in Daria's words echoed through the room.

The doctor shook her head and gave Daria a disapproving smirk as she picked up her belongings and turned to leave. Daria sat quietly, trying to calm her emotions while she held her new little boy.

Checking him from head to toe, she whispered, "Welcome to the world, little man. We gotta stick together, you and me."

She brought him up to her face and kissed his little head. "I already love you so much, even after everything we've been through. I wouldn't change a thing if it led me to you! Now we just have to find a way to get back to your daddy."

With her newborn son cradled in her arms, Daria couldn't help but reflect on the journey that had brought them to this moment. As she watched him sleep, a memory resurfaced, one that marked a turning point in her relationship with Jet.

Chapter Thirteen

Caught in Love

(2000)

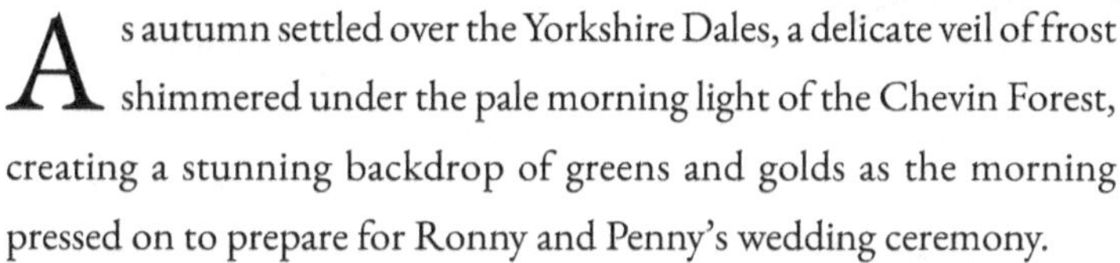

As autumn settled over the Yorkshire Dales, a delicate veil of frost shimmered under the pale morning light of the Chevin Forest, creating a stunning backdrop of greens and golds as the morning pressed on to prepare for Ronny and Penny's wedding ceremony.

Noon rolled around and, with the decorations finished and tables set, all the girls in the bridal party settled back at Penny's childhood home in Otley to get ready.

Penny, with her platinum blond locks and striking blue eyes, had grown close to Lily over the years. So, it was no surprise when she asked the sixteen-year-old to be a bridesmaid.

Lily watched as the others did their hair and makeup. Penny was ready except for her dress, so she came and sat next to her.

"Do you want to borrow some of my makeup?"

"No, I wouldn't know what to do with it, anyway." She shrugged.

"I know your Grandpa's a bit old-fashioned and doesn't like you to wear it, but today is a special occasion. I don't think he'd mind." She leaned over, whispering in her ear. "Besides, he'll never know. We can wash it off before you go home."

Lily's eyes lit up. "Could you help me?"

"Of course … Ladies?"

Penny and the other girls took turns. One had a pair of tweezers in her hand. "Do you know how long I have wanted to get a hold of your brows?" They all laughed.

"What's the matter with my brows?" Plucking away, she looked down at her and said, "Nothing if you want to look like a brute."

Penny defended her. "Oh stop, you wish you had those brows; they just need a little cleaning up ... Lily doesn't know how pretty she is because Jet keeps beating those boys off with a stick!"

"You're right about that." They all said together and got back to work, giggling.

"I don't want to catch any boys," Lily said, head back, wincing with every pluck. One of the other girls quipped, "Well after we get done with you today, he's gonna have to get a bigger stick because every boy at the reception will be chasing you."

Sitting next to Lily, Penny rubbed her arm, winked at the girl, and then left to get some makeup from her bag.

When they finished, they stood back and marveled at their creation. One of the girls held up a mirror in front of Lily. She began to tear up. Penny quickly grabbed a tissue and handed it to her. "What's the matter, Hun, don't you like it?"

She stood behind Lily, looking in the mirror at her. "I'm pretty ... I look like all of you now."

"Awe, Honey." She gave her a pouty smile and squeezed her shoulders. "Don't cry; you're gonna make the rest of us cry, and we still have a whole day to get through!" They laughed together instead.

At the church, everyone was seated, and it was time for the girls to be escorted down the aisle by the groomsmen. Lily's groomsman was Reggie, the drummer. An Irish native with shoulder-length hair the color of rust and large, pale blue eyes that slanted downward, even when he smiled. The freckles across his nose were barely visible on most days, as his usual two-day growth took the main stage.

But today, he was clean-shaven and hair combed, and Lily spotted them right away. He was only a year older than her, and he had conceded to being her escort for the entire evening. As she stepped out to greet him, his eyes widened as he inspected her from head to toe. "Lily? Look at you! You're all grown up!" She blushed as he proudly offered his arm, and they began their walk down the aisle.

Jet was Ronny's best man, and the two were already standing at the altar, looking back down the aisle. Lily saw Jet first and smiled, but his attention was on someone in the first row—likely his new girlfriend, Sarah.

Lily thought he looked so handsome in his tuxedo, even if his hair was a little too long for the occasion. As she made her way down the aisle, moving closer to Jet with every step, she imagined him as the groom and her as the bride being led by her grandfather to their very own altar.

As Lily drew nearer, Ronny discreetly nudged Jet, prompting him to look up. Initially caught off guard, his expression swiftly morphed from shock to confusion, and then to recognition as he realized who was approaching. *Wait … is that… Lily?!* His internal alarm bells rang, a flurry of silent protests tumbling through his mind. *What the hell is she … no … no, no, no, no. She's only …* His frustration was unmistakable. As Lily continued her approach, Jet closed his eyes, a sign of resignation to the unfolding scenario.

Lily had been hoping to impress him with her appearance. She thought, if anything, he would be happy if she looked closer to his age. But his reaction was almost heartbreaking as she noticed his obvious disapproval. Realizing that her efforts had been in vain, she fixed her gaze on the ground as she walked past him to her spot.

Ronny cast a sideways glance at Jet and nudged him again. Caught in the act, Jet became acutely aware of his less-than-stellar reaction being noticed. Drawing in a deep breath, he quickly straightened his posture and tried to regain his composure.

Lily didn't look at him again throughout the rest of the ceremony. However, he could not take his eyes off her. A silent testament to the unresolved tension and unspoken thoughts that lingered between them.

As the evening progressed, Reggie, who had been Lily's companion and escort for the occasion, sat with her through the speeches and dinner. When the actual party and dancing started, and they were free to roam around and mingle, Reggie went to get them some drinks.

Jet saw her alone and seized the moment to walk over, pull out a chair, and plop down in front of her. His expression and the gravity in his approach hinted at the seriousness of the discussion that was about to unfold. "What's all this?" He smugly pointed in a circle, indicating her face.

"What's what?" she snarked, glaring at his betrayal. He had always been her defender, but as of late, he had shifted into the role of attacker.

He leaned back in the chair and looked around. "Everyone is watching you, ya know?"

"Nooo, they're watching *you*!" Matching his attitude. "And instead of coming over to say hello or hey, you look nice tonight, you choose to come over and chastise me for what? Dressing up for a special occasion."

He glared at her, deep down knowing she was right, but ... "The way you look... It's like.."

"Like what?" she hissed.

He sighed, then leaned in, gritting his teeth, "I'm going to have to watch you all night now."

"What? Why would you have to do that?"

"Because they're already talking, Lily!" He leaned back in the chair, crossing his arms and shaking his head.

"About what? You're being ridiculous, Jet."

"You, Lily. Some of these blokes don't know how old you are. They're talking about wanting to date you. And that's a nice way of saying what they're *really* thinking."

Exasperated, she retorted, "So, what's it to you? You don't have to watch me. You're not my father and certainly not my boyfriend!" She paused, hoping for a reaction from him, but his expression remained stony. "You don't even want anything to do with me lately," she added with a shrug, her eyes beginning to glisten. "Maybe it *is* time to start dating?" Her words were meant to provoke. "Besides, you were already dating at sixteen."

Whispering through clenched teeth, Jet shot back, "That's different, Lily! I wasn't a girl."

"That doesn't even make sense," she spat, then rose to walk away. He moved to block her path, grabbing her arm in the process.

She looked at his hand, glared up defiantly, and jerked her arm away.

Reggie caught the interaction and ran up to them. "Whoa, hey now." He stepped between them and patted Jet on the shoulder. "You left her with me tonight, son. I'll take care of her." He pointed to Sarah. "You have a date, and she looks pretty lonely." Jet glanced over to see Sarah standing nearby, her arms folded, observing the scene along with the other guests.

Jet glared back at Lily for a moment, then at Reggie, before stomping off toward Sarah.

"Are you okay?" Reggie asked, concern clear in his voice. He gently put his arm around her to guide her back to the table and noticed her shaking. "Are you cold?" Without hesitation, he took off his jacket and draped it around her shoulders.

"No, not really, but I'd like to get out of here if you don't mind?"

"Yeah, that was some scene, huh?"

She looked up at him, her eyes full of regret. "I'm sorry. I didn't mean to ruin your evening," she apologized as they made their way towards the door.

"You didn't ruin anything, Lovey. I'm having a great time. I'm with the prettiest girl in the room tonight!" He gave her a toothy smile.

"I'm sure the groom would disagree, but thank you," she replied, smiling at his compliment. *At least someone noticed.*

"Okay, the second prettiest girl," he conceded.

Before they could reach the door, Penny grabbed her and hugged her, then asked, "Are you leaving?"

"Yeah." All three looked over at Jet to see him staring back at them. "I think it's for the best."

Penny held her hand. "Oh, Hun, I'm so sorry. If I thought for one second, he would react this way, I never would have offered—"

"This is your day. Don't you worry about me." Lily pulled Penny in to kiss her cheek and said, "It's not your fault he's being an ass."

Penny responded with an apologetic smile as Lily and Reggie walked out.

When they got to the car, Reggie opened the door for her. "What do you want to do? It's still early. We could go somewhere, or do you want to go home?"

"I don't care, I just need to get away from here ... whatever you want."

"Well, we're all dressed up, and I think we should take advantage of it," Reggie suggested.

Lily thought for a moment, then flashed him a bright-eyed smile and replied, "I think you're absolutely right."

As they arrived back in Leeds, they pulled up to a familiar neighborhood pub. Reggie parked the car and assisted Lily out before they made their way inside.

"HEY, Reggie!" The barkeep greeted them warmly as they entered. Reggie gave him a quick wave and a big smile as he led Lily over to a table. They took off their coats and sat down.

"How about something warm to drink?"

Lily nodded.

Reggie walked over to the bar and ordered. The barkeep asked, "Who's your new pet?"

Reggie leaned in over the bar and said, "That's Lily."

"No way ... what?" He squinted hard at her. "GAH, well, it's been nice knowing you! Does Jet know you got his girl out on the town?"

"She's not his girl; anyway, he's at Ronny's wedding with Sarah."

"Yeah, okay. Does he know you left with her?"

"Yeah." He sniffed. "I'm not afraid of him," he said smugly, then walked back over to Lily and sat beside her instead of across from her. They sat silent for a few moments, neither really knowing what to say.

Then, finally, the awkward silence was broken when someone brought a tray with their tea and a couple of sticky toffee puddings to the table.

"We missed the cake," he said, putting a plate in front of her as she poured her tea.

"You didn't have—"

"I'm your escort tonight. It would be ungentlemanly of me if I let you miss the cake. But this is the closest they had," Reggie quipped with a playful grimace.

She smiled gratefully. "Thank you for leaving with me. I don't know what's gotten into him lately. It's like he's always mad at me, and I don't know what I've done." She took a soothing sip of her tea, seeking comfort in its warmth.

"I do!" She looked over at him. "You grew up, and he's just realizing it."

"He sure doesn't treat me like I'm grown up."

"Lily, he still thinks of you as a little girl. He's afraid to think of you as a woman. If he did, he'd have to act on those feelings, and that scares the hell out of him, although he'd never admit it. Everyone knows he loves you, even if he doesn't. Besides, either way, your grandfather would kill him if he touched you." He laughed, then quickly added, "Well, now hang on; that might be good for the rest of us blokes who see you for what you are."

She rolled her eyes and took a big bite of her sticky toffee.

A few minutes later, Reggie and Lily were sharing a laugh at a joke the bartender had just shared with them when the door to the pub swung open. It was Jet. He strode over and stood at the table. "Get your things. I'm taking you home."

Reggie stood up and said, "I can take her home, Jet."

"Yeah, I bet you can."

"What is your problem tonight?"

Jet got right in his face. "You and the likes of—"

Lily stood, grabbed her things, and walked toward the door. Jet followed. She stopped short and turned around.

"I. Will. Get me home, thank you!" She glared at him, then leaned over and looked around him, saying in her most pleasant voice, "Thank you, Reggie, for a lovely evening." She then snarked, "Which is more than I can say for you!" She glared up at Jet, turned, and walked outside.

He followed her out while Reggie sat back down in defeat, throwing his napkin on the table.

Outside, Jet yelled for her to stop, "Lily!"

She ignored him, continuing to walk away, her heels clicking on the cobblestones.

"Lily!" he threatened louder.

She picked up the pace, more determined now. Then he shouted, "Daria Marie Daniels! Stop right now! I mean it!"

She stopped mid-stride. Tension hung in the air as she stood frozen, her back turned to him. He's never used this tone with her, and the use of her full name struck a chord. She was actually a little frightened. She didn't move or even turn to face him.

Jet approached her slowly, determination in each step. When he finally reached her, he grabbed her hand and pulled her to his car. He opened the door for her, and once she was settled, he slammed it shut, startling her.

When he got into the car, he put the key in the ignition but didn't turn it over. The air hung heavy with unspoken words, each passing moment intensifying the brewing storm, but he just sat there staring out the windshield. Lily stole a glance at Jet, uncertainty clouding her thoughts. Finally, he said, "Why didn't you go straight home?"

"Because it was still early, and we didn't want to waste being all dressed up … and we missed the cake, so—Jet, Reggie didn't do anything, if that's what you're worried about. He was a perfect gentleman the whole night." She sat back in her seat, put her hands in her lap, and then looked out the windshield. "You, on the other hand—why are you acting like this?" He ignored her this time, then turned the ignition over and drove to her great-uncle's house.

The hostility in the air was obvious as Lily's thoughts ran through the evening. Now she was angry. She had done nothing wrong after all, so why was he mad at her? Lily's attempt to decipher Jet's emotions continued to prove futile. Uncertain about how to mend what felt broken, she glanced over at him, a silent plea to the boy she loved. She wanted to—no; she needed to ease his mind. However, this was uncharted territory for them, leaving her with a sense of helplessness. So she remained silent.

Jet pulled up in front of her great-uncle's house and parked. He didn't get out, and when Lily grabbed for the handle, he reached over and stopped her from opening the door. The sound of their breathing filled the confined space for what felt like forever to Lily.

Finally, in a low, hoarse voice, he begged, "Lily." He sat back up and closed his eyes. "You have no idea what boys are like. They're gentlemen until they're not, and that can change in a heartbeat."

She tried to explain, "I'm not stupid. I don't flirt with boys. And I wasn't flirting with Reggie. We were just talking."

"Lily, you don't have to flirt with boys. You just have to … be you. You're sweet, and kind, and prettier than you believe … and they mistake that for flirtation. You don't even know you're doing it! When you're with me, you're with a much older crowd. They see you and think that you like them … and you do, but not like they like you. You're too good for all of these dodgy gits, anyway. Do you understand?" he asked, turning towards her. The sincerity of his voice contrasted with the earlier frustration, creating an air of guilt within her.

She turned her gaze away from him and sat staring at her lap, then softly said, "You make me sound like I'm some kind of china doll, like I'm too precious to touch."

"You are—to me," he croaked softly, his voice barely audible. She looked back over at him, his head bowed again. When he looked up and out the front window, his face was a mix of emotions, a storm of conflicting feelings that Lily still struggled to decipher.

She reached for him, her hand softly caressing his forearm, silently urging him to share his thoughts, as she turned toward him with concern.

He turned to her, their faces almost touching in the darkness. Leaning in, he cupped her cheeks, drawing her nearer until their foreheads met. "In case you haven't figured it out, I do want you, Lily. I fear I will always want you."

As he drew closer, her eyes closed, and she could feel his breath on her skin, a gentle warmth against the cool night air. His nose nestling against hers sent a shiver through her, as a tingle of anticipation coursed down her spine. Slowly and cautiously, his lips met hers, soft and warm, with a hint of tea and toffee.

Still holding her in place, he pressed a little more firmly; the sensation sending a rush of warmth through her. When she didn't pull away, he kissed her a little longer and a little deeper this time, his lips exploring hers with a tender urgency, igniting a spark of desire within her. Then, he whispered, "I could do that all night," his words a soft murmur against hers. She responded with a hum of contentment, her lips lingering against his. He dropped one hand while the other still held her, his thumb caressing her cheek with gentle strokes as he watched her face.

He grinned at her reaction, savoring the moment of shared intimacy. "Breathe, Lil," he teased gently.

Lily's eyes opened, meeting his. She took a deep breath that woke her from her daze and sighed. Jet pulled away, retreating into his seat, his gaze fixed downward.

"I can't do this anymore, Lil," he spoke so softly she barely heard him. He repeated himself, his words gaining a bit more volume. "I can't keep holding you at a distance like this. It's killing me." Jet's words hung in the air with a vulnerability that resonated within her. They were a stark contrast to the protective barrier he had always maintained. "I'm sorry about today. I know I was an ass, but I saw you walking down that aisle with Reggie; you looked so beautiful and grown up, and I got so ... I don't even know... jealous, maybe. I just couldn't imagine someone else walking you down that aisle."

"That's always been the plan," she whispered, her voice filled with a sense of relief and understanding.

He looked over at her, a grin spreading across his face. "I know—now. It's crazy! It's like we've been in this decade-long relationship, but it was always missing something," he mused, a realization dawning on him.

"You ... Jet. It was missing you."

"I know, but you can't blame—"

"Hey, I don't blame anyone. I'm just glad you see it now. I'm glad I can tell you how I feel without it sounding like the fantasies of a child."

Jet's eyes softened as he listened to Lily's heartfelt words. Her touch on his arm sent a comforting warmth through him. "You know, I have loved you from the moment you flounced down in front of me." He smiled in remembrance. "I looked up into those twelve-year-old eyes, and it was as if my soul came back to life. It had purpose and meaning again. And every second since, through every horrible thing, I've had a reason to push on." Her reminiscence of their shared history brought a tear and a tender smile to her.

"I'm sorry, Lily," Jet said softly, his voice laced with remorse as he remembered the childhood trauma that still, sometimes, lingered in her dreams.

"I guess I just needed you before you needed me ... fate's fickle timing and all," Lily mused, a hint of resignation in her voice.

Jet shook his head and let out a half-laugh. "Poor timing? That's an understatement. But I'm done. To hell with all of this age nonsense. We both know what we want."

Noticing the lights flicker on in the house, he tenderly lifted her hand and pressed her knuckles to his lips. "You should get inside." She watched his face as he spoke, looking for reassurance. "I'm staying with my parents tonight. I'll pick you up in the morning. We can go see Ronny and Penny off. I think I owe them an apology, too. Then we need to talk." She nodded and got out of the car, then walked on clouds all the way to her room, touching her lips and remembering their first kiss. The night held a sense of revelation and connection, a turning point for them both.

The following morning, Jet arrived to pick up Lily, and together, they embarked on the hour-long journey to Otley to bid farewell to Ronny and Penny before they left for their honeymoon. Afterward, they headed back to the garage flat. Engaging in small talk, they settled at the kitchen bar, the clinking of utensils and the hum of the kettle filling the air.

"Tea?"

"MMmm, love some."

Lily perched herself on a barstool while Jet took charge of preparing tea, the comforting routine providing a sense of normalcy amidst the impending conversation.

They were there to talk, but she had no idea when it would happen. Jet sat across from her at the kitchen bar, patiently waiting as Lily prepared her tea. She took longer than usual to make it just the way she liked it and unnecessarily cleaned her area—twice—and then sat quietly sipping from her cup.

Lily took long deliberate sips, collecting her thoughts before Jet broke the silence and asked, "How is it?"

"Good, thanks. Just what I needed."

Lily's anxiety was building, and she couldn't bear the tension that lingered in the air any longer. She shifted in her chair, fidgeting with the handle of her teacup. *Why isn't he saying anything?!*

The silence stretched between them, a stark departure from their usual ease of conversation. At least until recently, that is, but now things were different, and she could tell he found this conversation hard to start for some reason. *Well, if he's not going to start …* she cleared her throat and ventured, "So—"

"So, Lily … about last night," Jet interrupted, his tone serious as he set his cup down on the bar.

Her heart sank, and her face showed it. "You've changed your mind. Haven't you?" Her voice was barely above a whisper.

Jet walked over, turned her stool toward him, and stood between her knees to speak face-to-face. She grabbed the belt loops at his sides and gave him her full attention. Gently rubbing his knuckles against her cheek, moving a strand of hair away from her eyes. "I have not changed my mind. In fact, after spending the morning with you, I am even more convinced. But—"

"And there it is," she said under her breath.

He cocked his head, giving her a determined look, and, as if to show his resolve, he took hold of her face and pressed his lips against hers slowly and deliberately. His hands slid into her hair, fingers intertwining in the strands of her long curls, drawing her closer to him, kissing her with a definite sense of purpose. He was determined to communicate a heady message with this one simple act.

Her heart pounded through her shirt as the intensity of the kiss grew and stirred, pricking every pore in her body.

Her fingers, still clasping his belt loops, urged him closer, drawing him into her embrace. As she released her hold, her hands glided upwards beneath his untucked shirt, tracing the contours of his warm, smooth skin, ascending with a sense of urgency and desire.

Not trusting himself another second, he pulled away from her, releasing his grip and putting distance between them. He struggled to catch his breath before speaking. "But … we need some ground rules."

Lily, trying to recover, grumbled, "Ground rules? Like what?"

"Well," he cleared his throat and continued, "Number one, you have to be in charge."

"Ohhh, I like the sound of that." She perked up.

"I'm serious, Lily. You're still a little naive when it comes to … certain aspects of a relationship."

"You mean sex stuff? Yeah, I know all about that."

Cautiously, he stepped back into her grasp, lifting her chin to gaze at her suspiciously. Gradually regaining confidence in his self-control, he leaned in and gently nuzzled her forehead with his nose. Her eyes closed as she melted under his touch. Then, slowly and methodically, he continued to caress down the side of her cheek, then to her ear and neck, lingering while taking in her scent.

With a barely audible sigh, she corrected herself. "I mean … I haven't had it … yet … but the girls talk about it and tell me things." She sighed again as her head tilted back and to the side, accepting his exploration.

"Do they, now?" He grinned, his warm breath again sending shivers as he whispered into her ear, his lips grazing her skin with each word.

Moving back to her lips, speaking between each soft peck. "Well … what you hear … and what you experience … are two different things." Intertwining his hand in her hair once again, he kissed her deeply. His taste ignited a fire within her. As he pulled away, leaving her wanton, he continued to tease. His lips traced a path down her jawline, a trail of tingling sensations left behind. He stopped at her neck.

She sighed.

His tongue licked hot against her soft skin.

Her entire body went limp. Willing at this point to allow this man to do whatever he wanted.

He caught her, his arm wrapping around her, holding her upright.

Her head fell back as he continued his journey down to her chest, kissing and nuzzling just above her low-cut blouse. Instinctively, her hand rose to his shoulder, halting his advance. Her eyes fluttered open, searching for him, her breath hitching with anticipation.

He smiled, knowing he had proven his point, then kissed her softly. Jet paused, pulling away from her lips, his eyes locking with hers, his touch electrifying but serious. "I need you to know when to reign me in, Lil."

Completely relaxed in his grip, her breathing was jagged. "Mmmm ... but not from this, right?"

"No, not this." His breathing matched. "But you see now how this can lead to other things that I don't think you're ready for."

"I know." She nodded in his grip begrudgingly. He sat her up, and she took a deep, steading breath, acknowledging his lesson.

"But this I like." She wiggled a little in her seat to steady herself. "So, can we please continue?" He shook his head in disbelief. "Please, Lily, be serious. I would never forgive myself if I hurt you in some way."

"Alright, I get it." Her shoulders dropped in defeat, and she laid her head back with a pout. "What else?" she whined a little, wanting him to hurry and continue kissing her.

He grabbed her again playfully, laying her back in his arms and gave her a quick peck, trying to think of something else. "Uh ... that's it, I guess ..." He laughed. "Pops always said we were like an old married couple. So, I guess everything else is covered." He sat her back up and rested his hands on her shoulders.

They watched as Reggie came down the stairs. Half asleep and only wearing his pajama bottoms, he stopped dead in his tracks when he saw the two of them. "Oy, what's all this?" He rubbed his eyes and took a closer look at them.

Jet and Lily looked at each other and smiled. "Hey, sorry about last night."

Confused, Reggie pointed between the two. "Wait … are you two …" They smiled again. "Oh, thank God!" Talking to Lily as he walked to the refrigerator. "Do you have any idea what a twat this git has been!"

He looked at her, hiding his mouth behind his hand, and joked, "If I had known taking you out would make him move his arse, I would have done it months ago!" He winked at her, then rolled his eyes back.

She giggled, though Jet wasn't exactly pleased at being the butt of the joke. "Alright, Alright. We haven't told anyone yet, so keep it quiet till I can talk to her grandfather."

Reggie and Lily looked at each other and grimaced. As Reggie's playful jest settled between them, Lily couldn't shake the weight of what lay ahead—the inevitable conversation with her grandfather.

Chapter Fourteen

Opportunities

(2005)

After Jack's birth, Daria's days on the farm blurred into weeks, which turned into months, and then into years. Throughout this time, Uncle and Levi kept a pretty tight leash on Daria's whereabouts, keeping her close to the farm. Her sense of self gradually eroded, leaving her mired in depression. She spent her days just going through the motions, pushing herself to only take on the tasks and chores that were absolutely necessary.

Until one day, when Jack was two, Daria tried yet again to return to her home and Jet. Levi had been out all day, and that evening, a deputy sheriff pulled up in their truck, followed by a squad car. Daria glanced out the window, her heart pounding as she saw the deputy approach the house. When she opened the door, he tipped his hat and said, "Howdy, Ma'am."

"Where is Levi?" Her tone mixed with irritation and concern.

"Ma'am, Mr. Stratton is gonna be spendin' a few days' with us," the deputy replied.

"What happened?"

"Well, it seems your husband and one of the Dugger boys got into some trouble over at the Hoot 'N' Holler."

"What kind of trouble?"

"Well, uh ... he and Paul's boy were... um—"

"Just spit it out, deputy. I know what kind of man he is." Irritation now clear in her voice.

"Well, ma'am, they had been drinking most of the afternoon and got into a fight … over Janie, Sal's waitress. Sal don't mind a bit of roughhousin', but these two boys were really goin' at it. And Levi, well, he just wasn't lettin' up."

"*Of* course not," she said dryly. "Do I need to bail him out?"

"No, ma'am. No one is pressing any charges, but the sheriff wants him to dry out. Teach 'em a lesson. Will you and your boy be okay out here on your own?"

Daria's mind raced, her frustration transforming into a spark of opportunity. She could see the chance she'd been waiting for.

"Um, a few days, you say?"

"Yes, ma'am."

"Yeah, of course, we'll be fine."

The deputy dropped the truck keys into Daria's hand, tipped his hat again, and nodded goodbye. As he walked away, Daria's irritation faded into a determined resolve.

She stood at the door, Jack now on her hip, as the deputy got into the passenger side of the squad car and rode off. This unexpected turn of events could be just the break she needed.

The minute they were out of sight, Daria's heart raced with a mix of fear and exhilaration. She rushed into the house, her hands trembling as she put Jack in his playpen. With a sense of urgency, she packed bags for both of them and threw the bags into the truck.

Realizing she would need more money, Daria felt a pang of anxiety. She had a little bit of her own cash stashed from grocery trips, but it wasn't nearly enough to get out of the state. Determined, she scrambled through Levi's room, desperately searching for anything that could help.

Once in Levi's closet, she looked through his pants pockets, coats, and dresser. She discovered an envelope in the back of his sock drawer with more cash and a credit card. She couldn't believe her luck. After all, that was the one thing she had very little of, but she was gonna take what she could get, so she grabbed Jack, and they took off.

It had been almost three years since she had driven a vehicle, but as the old saying goes, it's just like riding a bike, right? When she got to the edge of their long dirt driveway, her heart pounded in her chest as she sat there staring in both directions, not waiting for traffic but for someone to stop her.

This was too easy, almost like a trap. Daria sat there for nearly two minutes, her breath shallow, waiting for the proverbial anvil to drop. When it didn't, she took a deep, steadying breath, gripping the steering wheel tightly, and made a left-hand turn away from town. Her destination—anywhere but there.

Daria drove into the night, heading west, and was almost out of Kentucky. Needing gas, food, and rest, she took care of the first two, then found a little out-of-the-way strip motel on the side of the road.

Daria settled into the motel, using the credit card she had found in Levi's sock drawer to pay for the room. It felt like a small victory, but she knew she had to be cautious.

Jack woke her up the next day earlier than she would've liked, but she knew she needed to get going. She packed up their things and continued driving west, her mind racing with thoughts of freedom and the life she hoped to rebuild.

For the next two days, she kept a low profile, using the credit card only for gas and occasional meals. She avoided major highways and stuck to winding back roads, hoping to stay off the radar. Every turn and every stop was calculated, only using the card at places that seemed less likely to be connected to a network.

Daria figured that when Levi got home, and she, Jack and the truck were nowhere to be found, he would report it to Uncle. What she didn't know was how soon Levi would discover the card was missing. It was pretty quick, setting off a chain of events that led Uncle right to her.

The next evening, after a long day of driving, Daria pulled into a small diner on the outskirts of a sleepy little town. She ordered a modest meal for herself and Jack, trying to maintain a sense of normalcy for her son. As she handed over the credit card to pay, the cashier excused himself and disappeared into the back, where he made a quick phone call to verify the card.

States away, Uncle received an alert about the card's usage. His contacts had been monitoring the card for any activity, and this latest batch of transactions gave away Daria's direction and her newest location. He immediately set out to find her, determined to bring her back.

As Daria packed the car to leave a motel a day later, she noticed the familiar black Lincoln pulling into the parking lot. Her heart sank as she recognized Uncle stepping out of the vehicle, his face a mask of determination.

"Daria!" he called out, striding toward her, Giles and the doctor not far behind.

Daria stood silent, wanting to scream but holding it in for Jack's sake. Her anxiety churned beneath the surface, her fists clenched tight to Jack's car seat. Uncle and Giles took positions at the front and rear of the truck in case she ran, their faces stony. She found their caution absurd—she would never leave Jack alone with them, not for anything.

The doctor approached her first, her tone laced with a cold, mocking curiosity. "Did you enjoy your little vacation?"

Daria sneered at her. The look cold and piercing, as if she were looking straight through her target, leaving no doubt about the depth of her disdain.

"I hope we do not have to sedate you this time."

Daria looked the doctor up and down, her gaze searching for any sign of a needle or other threat. "No, you don't," she said, her voice barely above a whisper.

"Good," the doctor replied with a smirk, taking Jack from his car seat with a practiced ease. She turned and walked back toward the Lincoln. Daria followed, her movements resigned to her fate, as she dropped the keys into Giles' waiting hand.

The ride back to Kentucky from Utah was a tense, and mostly silent, affair. Uncle and the doctor maintained a steely silence, their expressions revealing nothing of their thoughts or intentions. Daria's mind raced, filled with despair again, longing for Jet. She stole glances at Jack, who slept fitfully in his car seat, the innocence of his slumber a stark contrast to the turmoil roiling within her.

As they merged onto the county road leading to her and Levi's homestead, Uncle finally broke the silence. "What was your plan, Daria?"

She ignored him, but in her mind, she had run through all the potential scenarios for her escape. Her plan was to find a small town to disappear into, get a job, and save enough money to return home. Simple, right?

Except she didn't have a passport, visa, or a support system for Jack. She couldn't contact anyone because all the phone numbers in England had changed. Legally, at least on paper, in the US Jack was Levi's son, and leaving the country without Levi's permission or if he reported Jack as abducted would mean losing him altogether. Unfortunately, being young and sheltered, Daria hadn't fully grasped the logistical challenges she would face.

Uncle spoke again, bringing her back into the conversation. "You know, running was a mistake. You're lucky we found you before something worse happened."

Daria glared at him, her voice trembling with suppressed rage. "Lucky? You think I'm lucky? I just want to be with Jet, to have a life free from all of this."

Uncle's eyes flicked to the rearview mirror, meeting hers with a hard, unyielding gaze. "John is out of the question. You belong with your family, where you're safe."

"Safe?" Daria spat, her voice rising. "Safe from what? I was safe in England, I'm not safe here! Nor is Jack! We're not safe with a man who doesn't care about us?"

The doctor turned slightly in her seat, her expression inscrutable. "You need to accept your place, Daria. The more you resist, the harder it gets."

Daria turned her gaze to the passing scenery, her heart sinking with each mile that brought her closer to the farm and further from her true home. The countryside blurred through her tears as she whispered, "I don't belong here. I belong there with him."

The doctor, sitting in the passenger seat, glanced back at her, her face a mask of clinical detachment. "You need to think about what's best for Jack. Stability is important for a child."

Daria's eyes flashed with anger. "Don't you dare talk to me about what's best for my son! None of you care about what's best for him or for me. This is about control, about keeping me under your thumb. And you don't even have the decency to tell me why!"

Uncle's grip on the steering wheel tightened. "Enough, Daria. You need to come to terms with reality. John is in the past. Focus on your son and the life you can build here."

Daria fell silent, her thoughts a chaotic whirl of hopelessness and defiance. As they pulled into the familiar driveway of her little homestead, tears streamed down her face. The sight of the place reminded her it was her prison, each familiar detail confirming the life she was being forced back into.

As the car came to a stop, Uncle turned to her one last time. "Make peace with this, Daria. For Jack's sake."

She didn't respond, her silence a final act of rebellion. She stepped out of the car, lifting Jack into her arms, her heart heavy with shattered dreams and a future she couldn't bear to face.

Levi stood by the front porch, arms crossed and a smug grin spreading across his face. His eyes gleamed with satisfaction, relishing her return and the defeat etched in her expression. He reveled in the power he held over her, his posture exuding arrogance and triumph. Every step she took towards the house only fueled his gloating demeanor, as if her misery was his ultimate victory.

As if having to come back to this prison wasn't enough, eight days later, Giles, Uncle, and the doctor returned. They had her sit on the couch as they stood over her.

"We were unsure of how to punish you for your latest excursion," Uncle said, handing Daria a small square box, unwrapped but closed with a red ribbon tied into a bow. "We believe this will show you how serious we are about your situation."

Daria, confused, took the box. "Open it."

Her hands trembled as she untied the ribbon and lifted the lid. Inside, she found something that made her blood run cold—a severed ear. Recognition hit her like a freight train. It was her grandfather's ear, the familiar, distinctive mole on the lobe unmistakable. She looked up at Uncle, horror and disbelief in her eyes as she dropped the box to the floor.

Uncle's expression, stern and unyielding. "This is what happens when you try to run."

Tears streamed down her cheeks, and she couldn't breathe or even speak. Daria's mind raced, a torrent of emotions—fear, anger, desperation—overwhelming her. "You're a monster," she croaked after gasping for breath.

"We are very serious," Uncle replied, his tone devoid of any compassion. "You can't escape, Daria. You belong here, and you will never find your way back to John. Unless you would like a matching set. You must accept it."

The room spun, suffocating her as his words assailed her. Daria clenched her fists, but she knew she had to stay calm and strong for Jack, even though the reality of her situation was almost too much to bear. Then, the doctor walked out of the bedroom with Jack in her arms and a packed bag.

"Jack will be coming home with us," Uncle informed her.

That was it. Something snapped inside her. With a primal scream, Daria lunged at Uncle, her fists flying. Her nails clawed at his face. She landed several blows before Levi and Giles could react. She went wild, fueled by a mother's desperate fury and an overwhelming need to protect her child.

Uncle stumbled back, trying to shield himself from her relentless assault as Levi and Giles sprang into action, pulling Daria away from him. She fought them with everything she had, her strength sustained by sheer rage. It took both men to drag her to a chair and pin her down, her chest heaving with exertion, eyes blazing with an uncontained storm.

Uncle wiped his face with his handkerchief, smearing blood across his cheek. He stood in front of her and smiled. He gave Giles a knowing look, then just under his breath, he muttered, "She'll do."

Ten days later, Uncle and the doctor returned with Jack. Daria was inside when she heard the familiar rumble of the Lincoln pulling up. Her heart leapt as she burst through the front door, sprinting toward the car. Before they could even open the doors, she was there, frantically pulling on the handles.

"Unlock it!" she shouted, her voice breaking with desperation.

She heard the click of the lock opening and wasted no time. She yanked open the door and grabbed Jack out of the car seat, clutching him tightly to her chest. "Hi, baby," she whispered to him. Tears of relief streamed down her face as she held him close, feeling his warmth and hearing his small, confused murmurs.

"Mommy missed you so much." Her voice choked with emotion. She glanced up, her eyes narrowing as she looked at Uncle and the doctor. "If you ever take him away from me again—"

Uncle raised a hand to stop her. "This is your last chance, Daria. Don't make us regret it."

She glared at him, the fire of determination burning in her eyes. "I won't let you take him. I will find a way to kill you if it's the last thing I ever do."

The doctor stepped forward, her expression cold and clinical. "Remember our deal. If you want to keep him, you must comply."

Daria's grip on Jack tightened. She would play along for now, for Jack's sake, she would endure anything.

When things calmed down and life on the farm was getting back into a routine, the doctor came by and picked Daria and Jack up.

"You will come with me today."

"Where are we going?"

"You will see."

As they drove to the other side of the mountain, Daria wondered what this trip was all about. When they arrived at their destination, the doctor told her to follow her. The location was a large warehouse of sorts. No distinguishing marks or signage gave any indication as to what they were walking into.

Daria held Jack tight as they entered this massive metal building, now realizing the warehouse was an expansive gym, but unlike any other she had ever seen. Eerie and utilitarian in design, someone, most likely Uncle, had converted it into a clandestine training facility. The dim, industrial lighting cast dark shadows, giving the space a foreboding atmosphere. Concrete floors, walls lined with chain-link fences, and exposed metal beams added to the stark, prison-like feel.

In one corner, there was a meticulously crafted mock-up of a suburban house. Complete with furnished rooms, most likely designed for close-quarters combat training. Opposite the house, a simulated office space stood, filled with cubicles, desks, and computers, all arranged to provide a realistic environment for tactical drills.

Adjacent to these areas was a gun range, its walls padded and reinforced to contain the noise and stray bullets. Targets of varying shapes and sizes were set up at different distances on the gun range, some stationary and others on tracks to simulate moving threats.

Scattered throughout the warehouse were various types of gym equipment—treadmills, free weights, and punching bags—but interspersed with more unusual gear. There were climbing ropes, obstacle courses, and even a small climbing wall. One section featured mannequins dressed as different adversaries, used for practicing disarming and takedown techniques.

The entire setup resembled a scene from a spy thriller, with everything ready to prepare someone for high-stakes, real-world scenarios. She half expected Q to walk up and hand her an ink-pen phone or some other gadget used for espionage. But the sweat and metal wafting through her senses made the air thick, and the occasional sound of gunfire or the thud of bodies hitting mats punctuated the otherwise heavy silence.

Daria and Jack followed the doctor into an upstairs observatory and office space where Uncle was sitting behind a desk, waiting. He stood when they entered and gestured for the group to sit. The doctor walked around the desk and stood by Uncle, as Daria found her seat.

"What do you think of the place, Daria?" His voice was smooth and controlled.

"I think I'm confused. Why am I here?"

"If I recall correctly, you threatened to kill me. If that is something you are planning, you need to be better at it than me," Uncle replied with a faint smile.

Daria rolled her eyes. "I thought you were taking Jack away from me."

"Oh, he will be making more trips with me in the future." Daria's eyes narrowed. "Yes, he will be my insurance so I can visit family and not have to worry about you running again. But you showed promise that day, and I believe you have the potential to work with me and my team."

"What do you mean, work with your team? I'm a girl, not a gangster!"

"Is that what you think of me?" A hint of amusement in his voice.

"Well, given our history," she shot back.

"I guess I could see that. But I assure you, Daria, I am nothing more than a businessman looking to protect my assets," Uncle said, his tone turning serious.

"Is that what me and Jack are—assets?" Her voice was tight with anger.

Uncle took a moment to think and then said, "My most precious."

That took Daria aback. She was dumbfounded. How was she supposed to react to that?

Uncle, realizing her surprise at his statement, continued, "The offer is on the table. When you are ready, the position is yours."

The room fell silent, his words still reverberating in her mind. Daria looked at Jack, then back at Uncle, her mind racing with conflicting emotions. She knew she needed time to process everything, but one thing was clear—her life was no longer her own. It hadn't been for some time now, but perhaps, just maybe, at some point, there was a way to turn this to her advantage.

Chapter Fifteen

Permission

(2000)

It was a regular Wednesday evening at the Lovell's cozy terraced home. The Thomas family was over for dinner and cards. And even though Jet had his own place now, he would frequent these family dinners to see Lily. After dinner, Jet, Lily, and the women cleared the table while the men set up for the game. When Jet walked back into the dining room, he found the men still seated around the table. He paused, listening to the men's banter about who was getting ready to beat whom in tonight's game.

Wallace, noticing Jet standing still, called out, "John, are you staying for the game?"

Jet cleared his throat nervously. "Mr. Lovell, could I have a word with you?"

Wallace looked up, his sharp eyes narrowing slightly as he assessed Jet. He nodded, setting his cup down carefully on the saucer. "Mr. Lovell? Huh, this doesn't sound good." His eyes shifted to Frank, who shrugged, uncertain of his son's intention.

"In private, sir." Without needing to be asked, Abe and Frank got up and walked into the now-cramped kitchen with Lily and the women.

Wallace gestured for Jet to sit.

Jet began, "Mr. Lovell, I—"

"Wallace, son, no need to stand on formality around here."

"Wallace..." Jet accepted, then paused, gathering his thoughts. "I wanted to talk to you about Lily."

"Is there something wrong with Lily?"

"Oh, no sir. I ... I wanted to talk to you about ... I mean, ask your permission to ... see her."

Wallace studied Jet for a moment, his expression unreadable as the silence stretched between them. Finally, Wallace spoke, his voice steady but firm as he took his glasses off and placed them on the table.

"Is that what you kids call it these days? Seeing? Let me see if I have this straight. You want to court or date my granddaughter?"

"Uh, yes sir."

"Huh..." Wallace sat for another long moment, then said, "Well, I can't say this was an unexpected conversation, but I had hoped it would've come at a much later date."

Jet offered a grimaced smile.

Wallace let out a sigh. "Jet, you've always been a good lad, and I've seen how you've looked out for Lily over the years. But this is a serious matter. She's only sixteen, still finding her way. What makes you think you're ready for this, and more importantly, what makes you think she's ready?"

Jet swallowed, his resolve hardening. He met Wallace's gaze directly, his voice sincere. "I've thought about this a lot, sir. I wouldn't be here if I wasn't sure about how I feel. I know she's young, and that's why I wanted to come to you first. I don't want to do anything that would hurt her or make her life more difficult. But I also know that I love her, and I'm willing to wait, to be patient, to do things the right way."

Wallace's expression softened slightly at Jet's earnestness. He leaned back in his chair, contemplating Jet's words before responding. "I'm glad you came to me, Jet. It shows you respect our family and Lily. But understand this—Lily's future is important, and her happiness even more so. If you're serious about this, you'll need to prove it. You two have your whole lives ahead of you, and I won't see her rushed into anything she's not ready for."

"No, sir. I promise."

The room felt suddenly smaller as the distant hum of conversation drifted from the kitchen, Jet's focus entirely on the older man sitting across from him.

After a long pause, Wallace leaned forward, his tone becoming more serious. "Son, you understand what you're asking for, don't you? This isn't just about you and Lily having a bit of fun together. This is about her future, her well-being, her heart. If you care for her as much as you say, then you'll understand why I'm being cautious. Love isn't just about the good times, Jet. It's about the hard times too—the times when things aren't going your way, when life throws you a curveball, and you have to figure out how to handle it. It's about patience, sacrifice, and sometimes putting the other person's needs before your own. Are you prepared for that? Because she's not like a lot of other girls, Jet. There are things in her past that—"

"I know, sir. And maybe that's why, or maybe in spite of that, I feel the way I do about her. It's different with her—there are no walls, no pretense. She doesn't have to hide anything with me, and I don't have to fake who I am around her. It's just us; we just ... fit, if that makes sense."

Wallace settled back in his chair, the lines on his face deepening as he considered Jet's words.

Jet continued, "I know there will be challenges, but I'm ready to face them. For her."

Wallace sighed, a heavy sound that seemed to carry the weight of years of experience.

"All right, Jet. I'm not going to stand in the way of this, but ... you'll have to take things slow, show me that you're willing to be the man Lily deserves. Be patient, and most of all, make sure you're putting her best interests first. If you can do that, you'll have my blessing."

Jet felt a wave of relief wash over him, but he didn't allow himself to relax just yet.

"Thank you, Wallace. I promise I won't let you down."

Wallace reached across the table, extending his hand. Jet shook it firmly, the gesture sealing the understanding between them. It was more than just permission; it was an unspoken agreement that Jet would do everything in his power to protect and cherish Lily.

"All right then. Let's see where this goes. But remember, I'll be watching."

As Jet stood up to leave, Wallace's eyes softened slightly. Jet thought he could almost see a smile on Wallace's face.

"And Jet ... take care of her. She's special."

Jet nodded, his heart swelling with the significance of the moment.

"I know she is, sir. I will."

Jet walked out of the room and into the kitchen, the conversation echoing in his mind. He found Lily and gently took her hand. Together, they walked out the door to the back garden.

Wallace strolled into the kitchen a moment later, all eyes on him as he moved to the window, where the group could see Jet and Lily hugging on the back patio. The soft glow of the garden lights bathed them in a warm light, making the scene feel almost surreal. Jet had his arms around Lily, holding her close as they spoke in hushed tones, their connection palpable even from a distance.

Abe, breaking the silence, asked, "Well, what did he say?"

"He asked for my permission to court Lily," Wallace replied.

Minnie gasped softly, her hand going to her mouth, while Frank looked surprised but not entirely shocked.

"And? What did you tell him?" Sebina asked.

Wallace walked over to the small kitchen table, pulled out a chair, and sat down with a tired sigh. He rubbed a hand over his face before answering.

"I told him ... I told him I wouldn't stand in the way. But I made it clear he needs to take things slow, to be patient, and to put her happiness first. He seemed to understand what he's getting into, but time will tell."

Frank nodded slowly. "Jet's always been responsible where Lily is concerned, Wallace. I think he'll do right by her."

The women exchanged emotional glances, their hands reaching for each other in silent solidarity. Minnie croaked, "I think we need some wine."

Sebina nodded in agreement.

Abe looked around at the family, then out the window at Jet and Lily. "Are we ready for this?"

Wallace, shaking his head with an exasperated grin, replied, "Absolutely not."

Chapter Sixteen

Hard to Breathe

(2007)

The memories of Jet were becoming increasingly bittersweet as they stirred within her the same tumultuous emotions she had during the haunting nightmares of her youth, leaving a lingering taste of longing and regret.

As Jack reached age five, he became an eager little helper on the homestead, his youthful energy infusing each task with joy and wonder. While Daria and Levi toiled away on the farm, he would eagerly play by his mother's side, his laughter mingling with the sounds of nature. Yet, with each new milestone Jack achieved, Daria became increasingly discouraged that Jet was missing out on these precious moments.

One day, as Jack excitedly showed his mother a drawing he made, that familiar pang of sorrow pricked. Her child's bright eyes and the joy in his voice were reminiscent of Jet as a young man. She struggled with conflicting emotions, torn between cherishing her son's happiness and the bittersweet reminder of the man she loved.

Jack's face dropped, noticing his mother's sadness. "What's the matter mommy?"

Daria pulled Jack onto her lap, hugging him tightly. "You're so talented, sweetie," she said, her voice soft. "Mommy is just feeling a little down today. You know, you remind me of someone very special."

Jack looked back at her, innocence in his eyes. "Who, Mommy?"

Daria smiled through her emotions. "Someone I loved very much, Baby. But hey, you know what? You've got his smile and his spirit, and that makes me really happy. Now, tell me more about your drawing."

Jack hopped down and gave Daria a full account of the world he drew for her. She sat patiently, listening to Jack weave his tale, the whole time knowing that she would have to pick herself up by her proverbial bootstraps and finally let Jet go if she was to be any kind of mother to Jack. But how could she possibly do that, seeing him in her son's eyes every day?

Jack had become the sole beacon of light in Daria's once again dark world. Determined to keep her promise to herself, she reoriented her entire life around him. She had established a routine for her and Jack after dinner, which consisted of bubble baths and bedtime stories.

Due to the limited space in their house, with only two bedrooms available, Jack had to share a room with his mother. Despite lacking personal space, Daria created a cozy and playful environment for Jack in their little hideaway. She decorated the walls with Jack's drawings, hung colorful posters, and filled the shelves with toys and books.

Daria and Jack spent evenings together reading stories and playing games in their shared room. Daria enjoyed reading to Jack just as her grandmother read to her. His favorite book was "Fox In Socks" by Dr. Seuss. He found the tongue twisters entertaining and would giggle as his mother attempted to repeat them rhythmically. And each night, when the evening follies were over, she'd tuck Jack into bed, planting a gentle kiss on his forehead. "Goodnight, my little man. Dream big dreams."

Levi's days were mostly spent working the farm with notable efficiency, skills Daria assumed he picked up from his upbringing. In the beginning, she learned a great deal from him in that regard and was grateful for the knowledge he passed on. However, despite being a valuable source of instruction, Levi had become increasingly absent from the farm, leaving his makeshift family to fend for themselves. Sometimes to the detriment of their own safety. Levi's prolonged absences and the lack of communication with the outside world left Daria feeling even more isolated. They were left without a vehicle or phone, as Uncle still did not fully trust Daria with a house phone.

A case in point was the morning Rocket got spooked by a snake in his stall. Daria had gone out to see what the matter was when the horse reared up and knocked her to the ground, leaving her unconscious. Fortunately, she wasn't seriously injured, and Jack was able to help her get to the house.

When Levi finally came home, he had to leave again to call Uncle, who brought the doctor to check on her the following day.

But this had become a usual pattern for Levi. He would begin projects on the homestead and then pick a fight and leave Daria to either complete the task or abandon it for him to finish alone when he returned.

On another such occasion after coming home from an afternoon at the Hoot 'N' Holler, Levi stood in the doorway, his arms crossed, watching Daria as she sat at the kitchen table. She was staring down at a cup of tea that had long gone cold, trying to ignore the tension that thickened the air the moment he entered. His presence was stifling from the hostility that had been building between them for weeks.

"You think you're better than me, don't you?" Levi sneered, his voice laced with venom.

Daria ignored him, refusing to turn around and meet his gaze. She had learned that ignoring him was often the safest route. But tonight, she could feel his anger stealing the air from the room.

"I didn't say anything, Levi," she finally responded quietly, though her hands shook.

"Don't need to. It's all over your face." He took a step forward, his boots scuffed against the floor. "Always acting like you're too good for this life, for me."

She clenched her jaw, finally turning to face him. "I'm just trying to get through the day, Levi. That's all I want."

Levi's eyes narrowed. "Through the day, huh? Like I'm some kinda burden you gotta deal with?"

Daria took a deep breath and sighed. "You know it's not like that."

"Like hell it ain't!" he shouted, slamming his hand down on the table, making her jump. "You think I don't see the way you look at me? Like I'm trash under your feet!"

"That's enough!" she snapped, finally losing her composure. "I've done everything I can to keep the peace around here. I've tried to be friendly to you, but you—" Her voice trembled, "You're cruel, Levi. You have been from the start."

In a flash, Levi crossed the distance to her side of the table and grabbed her arm. "What did you say to me?"

Daria struggled, pulling back, but his grip was tight, digging into her skin. "Let go of me!" Trying to wrench free.

"Maybe if you weren't such a cold-hearted bitch, you'd know how to be grateful," Levi hissed, yanking her closer.

Without thinking, Daria lashed out with her free hand, shoving him hard in the chest, her body rising to stand as he stumbled back, surprised by her sudden reaction.

"Keep your hands off me!" she screamed, backing away as the chair scraped the floor behind her. Her heart pounding in her chest.

"You think you're tough now, huh? Think you can stand up to me? You ain't nothing without me. And Uncle ain't here to protect you." He slapped her across the face with the back of his hand, her head jerking to the side, knocking her back into the chair.

Daria's chest heaved with fury and fear as she held her cheek, but she refused to back down. Glaring up at him, she growled, "I don't need you. And I damn sure don't need him. You're not going to control me anymore." She rose from her chair to face him.

For a moment, they stood there, locked in a silent battle of wills, as Jack walked into the room. "Mommy?"

Both adults looked over at him. Daria moved closer to block her son as Levi turned and stormed out of the house with a disgusted grunt, slamming the door behind him.

As the silence fell over the room, Daria stood there, trembling, her cheek still stinging from the altercation. She had won this round, but she knew Levi wasn't the type of man to let things go.

For now, she breathed a sigh, dropping her shoulders, relieved to have a moment of peace.

Levi would also spend several nights a week away from the farm now that Daria had become more proficient at handling the farm, and that night was no different. Daria assumed he was finding what he needed elsewhere. Which was perfectly fine with her.

She expected him home at some point the next morning, but he never showed. That evening, Levi, still not home, she watched the late show on TV. To her surprise, the host announced the band following the commercial break.

"Stay tuned, folks, we've got Fractured Butterfly coming up after the break!"

No way! Could it be? Lo-and-behold, when the show continued, Jet, Ronny, and Reggie walked onto the stage. She couldn't believe it. It was him!

They were on tour and were being nominated for a Grammy. *Good for him.* She smiled through her tears and waited to hear them play. When the music started, she immediately recognized the melody. It was her song. It was the song he wrote for her, her favorite song to hum.

Before the song ended, Levi walked in to see her wet-faced, sitting on the couch.

"What's the matter with you?"

"Shhh. I'm trying to listen."

"Hey, I know that song. Ain't that that song you always sing?"

She just stared at him, not wanting to provoke an argument. He stared at the TV for another minute.

"That's him, ain't it?" She didn't answer.

He walked over to the TV and kicked the screen, knocking the television back into the wall. When it crashed to the floor, he turned to her and said, "You're mine now, whether you like it or not! I guess I'm gonna hafta prove it, huh!"

Daria watched as he stumbled toward her. She stood to escape, but he grabbed her before she could get past the coffee table. Levi threw her onto the couch, landing on her back. She tried to regain her balance and pull herself up and away from him, but he was fast, or maybe just a very determined drunk.

Her heart raced, a chaotic thrum in her chest as flashes of Rob's face intermingled with Levi's. Rob's eyes—cold, calculating—stared back at her, a twisted smirk tugging at the corners of his mouth, his gaze filled with the same predatory intent she remembered. The image would flicker, replaced by Levi's face, red with anger, lips curling into a sneer. The veins in his forehead pulsed as his jaw clenched in rage.

The two faces blurred together in her mind. One moment Rob's hard, cruel stare, the next, Levi's twisted fury. The flashes were relentless, disorienting her, their expressions merging, turning her fear into an all-consuming panic. Every blink brought a new surge of terror, as though the ghosts of her past and present were attacking her in unison.

He pinned her down, placing one hand on her chest and one knee between her legs. She grabbed the arm that was pressing with both hands and tried to push him off of her. She couldn't breathe. Disoriented and trying to process what was happening, a paralyzing terror eventually set in.

He leaned over her, using his entire weight to gain control. Once he steadied himself, he grabbed one of her hands, pulled it off his arm, and slammed it above her head. Then he snatched the other hand, slamming it up to meet the first.

The sound of her hands hitting the leather echoed in her ears as her body stretched and contorted, leaving her unable to escape his hold. His hands were large and callused. She could feel his scabrous flesh against her wrists as he held her down, and the scent of alcohol and sweat filled her nostrils as she struggled.

Hoping to distract him, she pleaded, "Levi, stop it! You're hurting me!" Daria caught the intent in his eyes as he glared down at her.

He grunted and smirked, relishing in her struggle.

What was she thinking? Her pleas never stopped him from hurting her before. She needed another strategy. "Levi, not here. Jack is asleep; let's go to your room!"

"Nah, this is good right here!"

That not working, she screamed, "Stop it! Levi ... Stop!" She struggled to free her hands, but he only needed one hand to hold both of hers.

He reached down with the other and pulled her nightgown up to expose her underwear. He looked back up at her face, and with another cruel grin, he said, "Yeah, Baby, you keep saying my name! I'm your husband! I'm gonna give you something to make you remember that!"

While he continued to restrain her, he used his free leg to kick the coffee table away from the couch. As it careened across the room, he let go of her hands.

Daria was free, and in an attempt to escape, she slapped and pushed at him, only managing to scratch his face as he quickly flipped her onto her stomach.

Panic rose in her as he yanked her legs off the edge of the couch, sending her knees plunging towards the floor and her face buried deep in the cushions.

Her wrists burned and ached from his prior grip, making it a struggle to push the cushions down so she could breathe. With his full weight pressing on her, and one hand firmly between her shoulder blades, he yanked her gown over her underwear and ripped at them. When they were gone, he threw what was left across the room.

Levi then dropped to his knees and grabbed her waist, pulling her back to him and halfway off the couch, allowing her knees to reach the floor. Dragging them apart, he held them there, straddled by his own. Daria immediately tried to push herself up to escape, but Levi grabbed one of her arms and pulled it behind her, pinning it to her back.

He humped against her several times, holding her hip and pushing her face further into the couch. Then, stretching over her body, his free hand reached around to her inner thigh, rubbing and cupping her mound.

He buried his face in her hair and breathed her in. "Damn, girl, you're so soft."

"You're disgusting, Get off me!" she cried, her voice muffled by the cushions. Beads of cold sweat formed over her as she trembled, sending her body into shock as she realized her fight was not winnable.

Levi pulled a hand back to unbuckle his pants and yanked them down, releasing his erection. She could feel the length of his rock-hard member as he pressed it against her backside.

With determination, Levi resolved to claim ownership of this woman, no matter the cost. She was his wife, and he would make sure she understood that, once and for all.

Once more, he reached around to grasp her flesh, his hand invading her with his fingers. Clumsily, he found the entrance and penetrated her with one violent, selfish thrust.

Triumphantly, he had finally taken possession of this woman that was promised to him. He wanted to take his time, enjoy the reward that he had just fought so hard for. His first several pumps were slow and almost thoughtful, but when he heard her cry out and catch her breath, it only reminded him of the resentment that still lingered, so defying all common courtesy; clutching her hips with both hands now, he pummeled her with a wrath of indignation.

Every thrust was vindication. Five years of restraint and frustration with a woman who was repulsed by his every touch or advance. Five years of having to raise another man's child. Five years of listening to her hum that damn song. And five years of watching her pine over that man was finally ending tonight. She was going to learn that her place was there, serving him quietly and obediently. And if he had to break her like a horse, all the better.

Daria continued to writhe relentlessly, her body straining against his control, every ounce of her strength seeming feeble against his overpowering grip. "Please," Daria gasped, her voice feigning. "Don't do this." Anger and fight now waning as tears welled. She pleaded, "I'm begging you, Levi, stop."

"Girl, when are you gonna learn, the more you fight the better I like it?"

Defeated, she reluctantly gave in to his trespass, her body lying motionless in a desperate attempt to avoid further harm.

When he finally ended his assault, he slumped over her, collapsing onto the floor beside her and leaning back against the couch.

She dragged herself up to sit on her legs and catch her breath as her nightgown fell back down.

Holding herself steady on the cushions, she took a few more deep breaths, assessed herself, and when she felt ready, she stood and headed to her room.

Proudly, Levi half laughed as she walked away and slurred, "Told you I'd make you forget him."

When she closed and locked the bedroom door, she turned to see Jack sitting in the dark on the edge of the bed. "Mommy?"

"Yes, baby?" she whispered through tears.

"Is Daddy mad at you again?"

"Shh, it's okay, Baby. Let's get you back into bed." She walked towards him.

"But I wanted a drink."

"Okay, I'll get you some water." She walked to the bathroom and grabbed the glass next to the sink. As it filled, she checked her wrists and face to see if any bruising had begun. She filled the glass about halfway, then brought it to Jack; he took it and then sat in thought before taking a couple of sips.

"Mommy, was Daddy trying to give you a baby?"

Horror filled her as she realized what he must have seen. *Oh God, was he watching?* "What? No, Baby, we were just playing around." She took the glass from him, setting it on the nightstand as Jack crawled back into the bed.

"Well, that's how the goats do it. Daddy showed me."

Tucking him under the covers. "Did he, now? I bet that was an interesting day." Trying to steer his thoughts towards something more pleasant.

"Yeah, when Daddy took me to the big farm to get hay, we saw goats and cows and some horses, too. Daddy, let me sit on one of the little horses."

"That sounds like so much fun. Maybe Mommy will go with you next time." She smiled and pushed a bang away from his face, then leaned in to kiss him goodnight.

Jack could see her tear-stained face from the light of the bathroom and grabbed her cheeks with his little hands, then looked right into her eyes. Determined, he told her, "Mommy, it will be ok. I will be big one day, and Daddy won't hurt you anymore."

"Oh, baby," she cried as she scooped him up and held him tight, rocking him as her thoughts raced.

The hatred for this man right now burned through her entire soul, not only for his violation of her, but for the fact that her son witnessed it. She wanted to kill him for that reason alone.

It would be so easy, she thought. All she had to do was wait for him to pass out. She could use the cast-iron skillet she used to make fried chicken for them on Sundays, or maybe she could pull a brick from the garden, or perhaps she could take her time and try to find the key to the gun cabinet—Still holding Jack in her arms, trying her best not to sob in front of him, she thought about what the consequence of those actions might be? Then, after thinking about it more, she realized Jack had already gone through enough trauma for one evening.

So, putting those thoughts aside, she tried to calm herself for Jack's sake. Laying him to sleep, she went into the bathroom to wash away as much of Levi as possible, knowing that no amount of soap and water could ever erase this encounter from her memory.

Determined never to let this happen again, she resolved to use every means available to protect herself and her child from him. She remembered Uncle's offer to work with him and his team. Now that Jack was in kindergarten, she would have the time. Since Uncle or Giles, and the doctor, took control of picking him up and bringing him home daily, she could talk to them tomorrow. Besides, she needed to see the doctor anyway to ensure she was physically okay and to make sure she didn't become pregnant. She couldn't imagine carrying this man's child.

As she undressed and stepped into the shower, she turned on the faucet to let warm water pour over her, hoping to soothe her senses. She closed her eyes and tried to focus on the sensation of the water droplets cascading down her body, but her mind kept wandering to Jet's face. Despite knowing that thinking of him was futile, she couldn't resist the temptation. He was her only source of comfort, and secretly, it was her way of defying Levi. Besides, there was no chance he would ever discover her small act of rebellion.

Jet was the last calming piece of her past she had left—the only thing that nobody could take from her. Even if she never saw him again, she still had his memory. She needed that right now. She needed to stop replaying the horrible events looping in her mind. Desperate to push them away, she focused on a happier memory: her and Jet's weekend on the beach in Filey.

Chapter Seventeen

Monday Morning

(2001)

During the summer holiday break, they traveled to Filey Beach in North Yorkshire to celebrate Lily's seventeenth birthday. Jet, Lily, and a group of friends—including Ronny, Penny, Reggie, and his muse of the week—chipped in to rent a cottage for the stay. After finishing work on Friday, they unloaded the van's equipment, packed up their luggage, and piled in for the hour-and-a-half drive.

They spent most of the weekend walking along the beach and, in the evenings, visiting pubs and bars. On Sunday night, they followed the same routine. After leaving the pub, they continued the party in the courtyard behind their cottage. Lily fell asleep while sitting on Jet's lap. When the party ended, Jet carried her to their bedroom and put her in bed. He undressed her down to her shirt and panties, then climbed in beside her.

Monday morning, still in bed, Lily woke first. Face to face, she lay quietly so as not to wake Jet. Although Lily had seen him sleeping before, she had never studied him this up close until this weekend. The morning light streaming through the sheers made his skin look pale, considering his olive tones.

Watching him intently, she traced every tiny freckle and facial hair with her eyes and marked each breath. She examined the curve of his lips, and remembering how soft they were, she ached to kiss them.

A curl of his dark brown hair fell over one eye, and even though his eyes were closed, she knew the color because their eyes matched. A pale green with a deep blue ring around the iris.

Laying this close, she could see the man he had become now, not the soft-faced boy she had met all those years ago. Even so, this was still the same face that helped her soul find peace. The face that calmed her during troubled times and the face she pulled from memory when she was alone and in need of comfort. Being this close, she was positive that this moment would forever burn his image into her memory and ensure her ability to never forget him.

Jet breathed deep and stretched to wake. His eyes opened to find her stare. He stretched again, wrapping his arms around her and pulling her close. His face now buried in her hair, he breathed her in. "How are you feeling?"

"Better than I should, I think."

He rolled onto his back, one arm under her head, the other over his eyes to shield the light, still trying to wake. Lily couldn't help herself. She needed to be close to him, to touch him. If she could, she wished she could bury herself within him. But that not being an option, she pulled herself over to lie next to him, resting her head on his shoulder and her hand on his mostly bare chest. Her fingers ran through his curls, twirling them as she listened to his heart beating.

He allowed her investigation, even as her hand traveled lower, following the trail of curls downward. When her finger circled his belly button, he snickered. "What are you doing, naughty girl?" He grabbed her hand, rolled her onto her back, and playfully attacked her neck, growling and nipping. She squealed and giggled, trying to escape his attack.

He pushed himself up to see her face. "What are you up to?"

She calmed herself, giving him a more serious look. "Of all the years we've known each other, I've never really seen … all of you."

"What do you mean?"

"I was watching you sleep and thinking about … us … I mean… even though we've changed clothes and stuff in front of each other, we've never really seen each other…"

He realized where this conversation was headed and smiled. "Hmmm, so you're curious?"

"Well, yeah, kinda." She shrugged. "Ya know, you've been with all those girls, so I suppose you've seen everything, but I've never really seen a …" She couldn't bring herself to actually say the word.

"There haven't been that many girls, Lily."

She ignored his defense with a look of, oh, really?

He continued, "Honestly, though, I never took the time to look, either. They were more of a means to an end, if you know what I mean. Plus, we were usually in the dark. So …"

"Well, still, you've seen more than I have."

He searched her eyes, then thought for a moment and gave her a sly grin. "Are you sure about this?"

She nodded.

"Everybody is different … ya know, shapes, sizes …"

"I know, but I don't care about everyone else. I love you, and I want to know you."

He paused again, still gazing into her eyes, questioning her intent. "Well, if I let you explore, will you let me explore?"

"I mean … if you want to."

Giving her another sly grin. "Hell yeah, I want to. So, where do you want to start?"

Her hands pressed against his chest, rolling him onto his back with ease. Then, turning onto her side, she propped herself up on one elbow. Keeping her eyes fixed on the muscular contours of his long torso, she used the back of her finger to trace down his side, almost to his boxers.

He smiled and quivered under her touch. Inspired by his reaction, she stopped, looked up at him, then pushed herself up to straddle his body, holding herself on all fours just above him.

Her long, sun-kissed mahogany hair spilled onto him as she pulled it over to one side. She kissed him slowly and deeply, then moved lower down his neck and then to his chest, kissing and inching her body downward. She stopped and sat up when she met the cloth of his waistband. Nervously, she looked up at him, raised her eyebrows, and then looked down towards her intended target. He gave a quick nod, then flashed her his signature crooked smile.

She cautiously retreated down his legs, gently tugging the fabric until she successfully removed them. Navigating her way back up, she encountered his mostly hard shaft. Gazing back up at him, seeking approval, he propped himself up on his elbows, grinning once more, granting his permission. She bit her bottom lip and gingerly took it into her hand.

Holding it, she ran her thumb up and down the side, analyzing the texture, and was surprised to feel how smooth and silky the skin was. *This feels so different from what I imagined,* a mix of curiosity and nervous excitement bubbling within her. Feeling unsure of her next move, she peered up at him, seeking guidance. With a reassuring touch, he took her hand in his and showed her how to stroke it, his fingers gently guiding hers in a patient and careful manner. *Okay, I can do this,* she reassured herself.

After a couple of example strokes, he let her take over. Instinctively, she rubbed over the tip with her thumb and squeezed; his head fell back, releasing a sharp breath as she continued. To her wonderment, it expanded and grew even harder with every stroke, and after a few more moments, he abruptly grabbed her hand mid-stride. She sucked in a worried breath. *What did I do?*

Her heart was pounding. She froze, loosening her grip, thinking she had done something wrong. He caught his breath, grasped her arms, and flipped her onto her back, then rolled on top of her.

Laying very still, she waited for him to chastise her. Instead, he rested his forehead on her chest and continued to recover. A moment later, he looked up, a determined glint in his eyes, and said, "My turn."

She had not seen this expression before. It felt very private, but she liked it and giggled. Jet had been very careful over the last year not to take things too far, but today was different; she was different.

From the beginning of this weekend, he almost didn't recognize his sweet Lily girl. What he saw was this beautiful young woman emerging. Fitting in more with the age of the group. Just the same, he paused to make sure, looking into her eyes one last time for any remnants of that little girl.

Her gaze, charged with arousal, assured him she was no longer there. And almost as if to bid farewell to his Lily Bit, he leaned in, leaving a tender kiss on her forehead, the tip of her nose, and then her lips.

Her hands caressed his chest, finding his broad, flexed shoulders, and pulled him closer. The intensity between them had become intoxicating as he continued kissing her, deeper and more impassioned; sucking her bottom lip, he pulled away as he moved down to her neck and stopped to roll onto his side.

As she lay beside him, trying not to dissolve into madness, he unfastened the buttons of her shirt. Carefully parting one side, revealing the shapely curve of her breast. A gentle caress followed, his hand cupping and then exerting the slightest pressure as his thumb traced circles over her supple, tawny nipple. Mesmerized, he took in the tempting vision of her body and observed her eyelids gently shutting as she surrendered to the sensation.

He pulled her shirt the rest of the way open to reveal her belly and ran his warm hand down her center, slowly reaching her underwear and sliding his hand in. She took a quick breath and held it.

"Are you okay?"

"Mmm hmmm."

As he withdrew, his thumb ran along the edge of her white cotton panties, tugging them down on one side. "Is this okay?" He breathed warm against her ear.

"Yes," she sighed, lifting her hips to allow him to pull them off, her soft moan of consent barely audible.

Rolling back on top of her, he spread her legs with his, pressing his body close. "You're so beautiful," he murmured, his lips tracing a slow path from her neck to her shoulders, then lower to her breasts. He sucked and teased, his mouth moving in rhythm with her shallow, erratic breaths.

Moving lower to her belly, he sat up on his knees, his hands sliding down to grasp her hips. "I wanna make you feel good, Lil," he murmured, his voice low and filled with need, as he pulled her down the sheets toward him.

"Okay," she responded, breathless.

He placed one hand on her belly just above her well-manicured pubic bone and inched his thumb lower until he found what he was looking for.

Circling his thumb around and around, he took in the sight of her as she writhed, grabbing the sheets with her fists. He smiled, knowing this beautiful creature was his, as he put two fingers in his mouth to wet them and gently inserted them through her already wet flesh. Almost immediately, her entire body convulsed as she let out a soft groan. "Oh, God..."

He stilled, feeling her jerk and squeeze around him, her inner core tightening. "I love watching you like this," he whispered, slowly pulling out, satisfied, knowing he had brought her to climax.

As she caught her breath, he worked his way back up to hover over her, kissing her deeply. "You're amazing," he whispered against her lips, his voice full of awe.

She smiled up at him, her hand coming up to cup his cheek. "No ... you are."

She wrapped her arms around his neck and pulled him down to lie on top of her. She felt the rigid length of him pressing against her already sensitive skin, and with a breathless plea, she whispered, "I wanna know what you feel like inside me."

"Are you sure?"

"Hmmm, yes, please." Still panting.

With that, he reached for the bedside drawer, pulling out a foil packet. As he opened it and rolled it on, his eyes searched hers for any hesitation. "Lily, are you sure?"

In a deliberate ambush, she hooked her legs around his waist, pulling him down, kissing him, her longing evident in her plea. "Now, please."

He obliged.

Jet groaned against her lips, the intensity of her desire matching his own. With a steady hand, he positioned himself at her entrance, his eyes locking onto hers, searching for any flicker of doubt. But all he saw was trust and desire.

With a slow and measured pace, he pushed forward, inch by inch, her warmth enveloping him as they both gasped at the sensation. He paused, giving her time to adjust, his forehead resting against hers as they shared a breath. "Tell me if you need me to stop."

She nodded against him. Her eyes closed, lost in the heady buzz that was now taking over her senses.

She tightened her hold on him, her nails slightly digging into his shoulders as she whispered back, "It's okay, Jet. I'm okay."

He needed no further encouragement. He began to move, each thrust deliberate, finding a rhythm that had them both teetering on the edge of control. Her breath hitched with every movement, her body responding to him in ways that left him breathless. "God ... You're perfect," he whispered, his voice thick with emotion.

They moved together, the world outside their connection fading until nothing else existed but the feel of their bodies, the sound of their mingled breaths, and the shared, rising tension between them.

With a final deep thrust, he felt her body tense beneath him, and she cried out, another climax sending her over the edge. He followed her, his release spilling into the barrier between them as he held her close, their bodies trembling in the aftermath.

For a long moment, they stayed like that, wrapped around each other, basking in the shared intimacy. He kissed her, soft brushes of his lips against hers as they both caught their breath. When he eventually pulled away, it was only far enough to look into her eyes, his thumb brushing tenderly across her cheek.

"I love you, Lil," he murmured, the words almost a vow, a promise of everything that was to come.

She smiled, her eyes glistening with the same emotion. "I love you too."

Completely sated and dizzy, he pulled out slowly. They lay silent beside one another for a few more heartbeats. Finally, he turned to look at her. Lily's eyes were closed, and she was smiling. He rolled to kiss her one last time before he got up, but she grabbed him and held him, not wanting him to leave her just yet.

Folding her into his arms, pulling her as close as he could, he buried himself into her hair. Breathing in her comforting floral scent, he confessed, "I never knew it was possible to feel like this about someone."

"I did." She beamed, finally releasing him.

Chapter Eighteen

The Mission

(2011)

Jack, ever perceptive for an eight-year-old, noticed subtle changes in his mother long before anyone else did. He couldn't remember the last time his mother laughed. Her eyes, once warm and bright every time she looked at him, now seemed distant, like she was looking past him instead of at him.

As they worked side by side in the garden this week, he watched her, noting how she moved slower than usual. He had mentioned his concern for her to Uncle one day as they rode home from school. Uncle told him he would handle it and not to worry. But today, as he watched her again, she seemed detached, as if every movement took more out of her than it should. The sun blazed in the midday sky as she stood to grab another packet of seeds. He looked up at her with concern in his eyes. "Are you okay, Mama? You seem ... different."

Daria's smile wavered before settling into place, a thin mask that barely reached her eyes. Her hand mechanically brushed through Jack's hair, devoid of its usual spirit, as if her only goal was to maintain her facade rather than offer him comfort.

"I'm fine, sweetheart. Just a little tired, that's all." Her voice was steady but lacking its usual warmth.

Jack, however, not convinced, continued to watch her closely, his young mind picking up on the tension she tried to mask. Daria felt

Jack's eyes on her, the impact of his unspoken questions squeezing her chest. Her throat tightened, and for a moment, she found it hard to breathe. Some days the weight of it all felt endless—a sinking that started in her chest and spread until even breathing felt like too much. How could she tell him that each day felt like she was sinking deeper into quicksand? The more she fought, the faster she sank? And how could she explain the storm raging in her heart to a child? The truth was too complex, too dark, so she remained silent, hoping he'd accept her answer, even though she feared the day he would see through her facade completely.

The next afternoon, Daria was in the barn, the familiar sounds and smells of the animals grounding her in the routine she had come to depend on. She ran her hands over the coarse fur of a calf, her mind elsewhere, lost in the simple rhythm of farm life. Levi was absent as usual these days and the barn was her refuge, a place where she could momentarily forget the burdens that weighed on her heart. Her world could be chaotic, but here, things made sense. It was a rare moment of peace, one that was shattered when the barn door creaked open. Daria froze, the calf's soft braying suddenly too loud in the heavy silence. Uncle's shadow stretched across the floor, swallowing the light as he stepped inside. The air grew thick, making it hard to breathe.

Uncle rarely visited the barn, and when he did, it was never without a reason. His presence alone filled the space with a tension that made Daria's muscles tighten in response. He walked toward her with that same measured stride she associated with bad news or chastisement. But today, something was different—his usual stiff demeanor seemed laced with an urgency she hadn't seen before.

"Daria." His voice was as clipped and controlled as ever. "I need you to come with me. We have a situation that requires your... particular set of skills."

Her heart stopped for a split second. Uncle and his team had trained her for the last few years, honing her abilities with a relentless precision. But she hadn't ever been asked to take part in an actual mission. This was new, unexpected, and it sent a ripple of unease through her.

"What kind of situation?" Trying to keep her voice steady. She couldn't afford to show fear, not to him.

Uncle's eyes, sharp and calculating, gave nothing away. "You'll find out soon enough. Be ready to leave in an hour."

"Who's watching Jack?" She stood her ground, not moving until she had a definitive answer.

"He will be staying with me until you return. The doctor will pick him up later."

She knew better than to argue. Uncle wasn't one for explanations, and any resistance would only invite consequences she wasn't willing to face. Nodding, she set aside her tools and began mentally preparing for whatever lay ahead. The thought of leaving the farm, even for a short while, filled her with a sense of dread she couldn't quite shake.

As she packed a small bag, her eyes drifted to where Jack was playing outside, his carefree laughter a stark contrast to the storm brewing inside her. The idea of leaving him behind, even temporarily, sent a pang through her chest. At least, she thought, Jack would not be staying with Levi. So, she pushed those feelings aside. She had no choice.

An hour later, Daria found herself in the passenger seat of Uncle's car, the farm quickly disappearing in the side-view mirror. The landscape outside blurred into a monotonous stream of green and gray as they drove, the silence between them heavy with unspoken questions and mounting tension. Uncle's hands gripped the wheel with the same intensity she had seen him use when driving her back to the farm after multiple escape attempts. Whatever this was, it wasn't just another training exercise.

Eventually, they reached the outskirts of a small, nondescript town, where a remote warehouse loomed in the distance. It was a hulking, decrepit structure, the kind of place that seemed to have been forgotten by time.

A group of men—Uncle's men—were waiting, their expressions hardened and cold, their eyes sharp as they appraised Daria with a mix of curiosity and skepticism. She was smaller than they expected, athletic but still slight in stature, a stark contrast to the large, muscled men surrounding her. They exchanged glances, some silently questioning whether she could handle what lay ahead. To them, she seemed out of place, too fragile for the world they lived in, even if her sharp gaze hinted at strength.

Daria eyed them back. These were the men she had watched train after her lessons from the observation level at the training facility, the men who had probably seen and done things she could only imagine, and their presence only heightened her sense of unease.

Uncle stepped out of the car, his demeanor shifting into something even more authoritative, if that was possible. He introduced Daria to the team leader, a tall, imposing figure named Viktor. Viktor looked her up and down, his expression unreadable, though his eyes seemed to linger on her with a hint of disdain.

"So, this is the one you've been training." His voice carried a slight sneer. "She better be worth it."

"She is," Uncle replied curtly, his tone leaving no room for doubt.

Viktor wasted no time outlining the mission. It was a retrieval OP. The operation would involve surveillance, infiltration, and the recovery of important information. As Viktor spoke, Daria felt a chill run down her spine. This was far more serious than anything she had ever been trained for, and the reality of it pressed down on her like a weight she wasn't sure she could carry.

When Viktor handed her a small, sleek pistol, her hands trembled slightly. She had trained with weapons, knew how to use them, but the cold metal in her grip felt different now, heavier with the implications of what she might have to do. Viktor noticed the tremor and sneered.

"If you can't handle it, you're no use to us," he said, his voice laced with contempt.

Daria gritted her teeth, forcing herself to steady her hands. "I can handle it." Her voice was firmer than she felt inside.

With that, the team moved out under the cover of night, slipping into the designated target area with a practiced ease that only came from experience. Daria's heart pounded in her chest as they approached their site—a rundown building that served as the storage facility for one of Uncle's rivals. The operation was about to begin, and she knew there was no turning back now. She found herself thrust into a world where her hesitation could be fatal, and she needed to prove, not just to Uncle and Viktor, but to herself, that she was capable of surviving it.

At that moment, Viktor released the team to their assigned positions. Daria stood waiting for her orders. "You're up," he said with a look of cold steel in his eyes.

"Up?'"

"This is your mission, you are the only one trained on this type of security system. You're lead on this. Retrieve the materials and get out—quickly!"

Her breath caught in her throat, heart pounding so loudly she was sure Viktor could hear it. Her hands clenched into fists at her sides, trying to ground herself as the floor seemed to tilt beneath her feet.

"Why are you still here!" He stared down at her.

She took a deep breath and gathered what strength she had left, then turned toward her target.

Once inside, Daria crouched low behind a stack of rusted metal crates, her breath steadying as she scanned the area. The abandoned warehouse was a labyrinth of shadows and decay, the perfect setting for the kind of operation she figured Uncle specialized in. Tonight, she was evidently leading his team, and though she tried to look confident and calm, a storm brewed within her. Each training mission like this one chipped away at her soul, knowing that at some point she would be called to action, but she couldn't let it show. Uncle demanded perfection, and she had learned to deliver.

Daria felt the weight of the team's trust on her shoulders as they waited for her signal while moonlight filtered through the broken windows, casting eerie patterns on the dusty floor. She signaled for them to stay back as she moved forward, her steps nearly silent on the cracked concrete. The tension in the air was thick, each creak of the aging building making her heart pound a little harder. But fear wasn't something she was supposed to feel anymore. They had tried to train it out of her and replace it with an icy determination. She was close, but this being her first mission, she was struggling to remember that.

The target was a small, high-security vault hidden deep within the warehouse, containing a package that Uncle wanted. He hadn't given her all the details—he never did—but Daria had learned to stop asking questions. She was a tool, a means to an end, and she knew it. The realization was bitter, but it also kept her sharp, kept her focused on what needed to be done.

She found the vault in a secluded corner, almost concealed behind a heavy wooden cabinet that had once been part of the warehouse's main office. It was a relic of the past, its paint peeling, and hinges rusted, yet it stood as a silent witness to the secrets it guarded. Daria knelt before it, pulling out a small electronic device from her pocket. Uncle had drilled her on its use until she could disarm the most sophisticated security systems in her sleep. Her fingers moved with practiced ease, connecting wires, overriding security protocols. The cold, unyielding surface of the steel door was a stark contrast to the warmth of the adrenaline coursing through her veins.

The lock clicked, and the vault door creaked open. Inside, wrapped in brown paper, was the package she was to retrieve. But as she reached for it, a sense of unease settled over her. This was too easy. There was no one here, no guards, no booby traps. Had Uncle wanted her to succeed, to see if she would follow through without question? This wasn't a mission, it was a test. But why?

She knew better than to hesitate. *Don't overthink it, Daria. Move!* With a deep breath, she pulled the package out and tucked it into her backpack. It was lighter than she expected. *Is it empty?* She was about to close the vault when something else caught her eye—an envelope tucked into the corner, barely visible in the dim light. It had her name on it. *What the hell? Is this the trap?* Against her better judgment, she grabbed it, slipping it into her jacket pocket without opening it.

Daria retraced her steps, moving with the same caution she had used to enter. The team was exactly where she had left them, waiting in the shadows. They fell in behind her as she led them out of the warehouse, the night air crisp and biting as they emerged into the open. She handed Viktor the package and they headed out the same way they came in.

The drive back to the farm was silent. The tension that had been so palpable earlier now replaced with a sense of relief and skepticism. Daria stared out the window, her mind racing. What was in the envelope? Why had it been left there, knowing she would find it? She was afraid to know, but the curiosity gnawed at her. She couldn't ignore it.

Once back at the farm, the team dispersed, each member returning to headquarters. Once she was alone, Daria lingered in the barn, the familiar smells of hay and livestock grounding her as she sat on a bale of hay, the envelope burning a hole in her pocket. With trembling hands, she pulled it out and carefully opened it.

Inside was a single sheet of paper, the words typed in neat, unassuming font:

You are not a tool, Daria. You are not what you believe we made you to be. You are still capable of love, of hope. Don't let this take that from you.

The note was unsigned, but Daria knew who had written it. Uncle. Her heart pounded as she read the words over and over, disbelief mixing with a faint glimmer of something she hadn't felt in a long time—hope. That word, that single paltry word, was bouncing around in her head. *Why would he write this?* Was this another one of his twisted tests? Or was there a part of him, buried deep beneath the layers of control and manipulation, that actually cared for her in some way?

Daria's thoughts were a tangled mess as she stared at the note, trying to make sense of it. Uncle had always been a complicated man, his motives never fully transparent. But this ... this was different. It was almost as if he was giving her some form of reassurance, a chance to reclaim something she thought was long lost.

But could she trust it? Could she trust him?

The barn was quiet. The only sound was the distant lowing of cows and the rustle of the wind through the rafters. Daria closed her eyes, letting the sounds wash over her as she tried to calm the storm inside her. She had spent so long building walls around her heart, walls that kept her safe but also kept her isolated. Was it possible that Uncle, the man who had molded her into what she was, was now offering her a way to tear those walls down?

The note crumpled in her hand as she clenched her fist, anger and confusion battling for dominance. She didn't want to hope, didn't want to believe that there was still something inside her worth saving. But the note was undeniable proof that someone, even if it was Uncle, thought otherwise.

Daria stood, shoving the note back into her pocket as she made her way out of the barn. She couldn't afford to think about this now, not with everything else on her mind. The farm, the training, the mission, Levi and the life she had been forced into became all she knew now. But as she walked toward the house, a small voice in the back of her mind whispered that maybe, just maybe, there was a different path she could take. A path that didn't involve missions or Uncle or the cold, empty life she had been living.

For now, though, she would keep the note close, a small reminder that there was still something human inside her, something that Uncle's training and control hadn't broken. And maybe, one day... some day... she would find the strength to follow that voice and break free from the life that had trapped her for so long.

But not today.

Today, she completed a mission. They assigned her a role, and she carried it out because that was who she was now.

Or at least, that was who he had made her to be. For now.

Chapter Nineteen

Make Up Quick
(2001)

Jet's fingers drummed impatiently on the steering wheel as he waited outside the small cafe where Lily worked. The late afternoon sun cast shadows across the car park. His jaw tightened with every passing minute. She was late again. That manager of hers, keeping her later and later after her shift.

Jet blew out an angry sigh, his gaze locked on the cafe door. *This is ridiculous. She has school tomorrow. Plus, I don't like the way that git looks at her. This ends today.*

The air outside felt thick and suffocating as Jet stepped out of the car and walked towards the cafe, his boots crunching against the gravel. He was just about to reach the door when it swung open, and Lily walked out, nearly colliding with him. Her face was flushed, her cheeks a soft pink, and her eyes darted nervously as she approached him. Without a word, she walked past him and climbed into the car, fastening her seatbelt, still avoiding Jet's gaze.

"You're late—again," Jet said, his voice sharp as he slid into the driver's seat.

Lily flinched but tried to keep her tone light, her voice thin. "I lost track of time. I was just—"

"Just what, Lil? Talking to that guy again?" Jet's words came out like a slap, the tension in the car thickening.

Lily's heart sank, an icy knot forming in her stomach. She turned to look out the window, her breath fogging the glass. "He's my boss, Jet. You know that."

Jet's eyes narrowed as he turned to face her, his expression hard, his knuckles white on the steering wheel. "Boss, huh? Is that why he's always calling you, always finding excuses to keep you late? I'm not stupid, Lily."

Her frustration bubbled over, her voice rising despite the tightness in her throat. "Why do you always do this? You act like I can't have friends or a life outside of you. I love you, Jet, but you can't control everything I do!"

"I'm not trying to control you," Jet shot back, his voice a low growl. "I just don't trust him. And I don't like the way you're always defending him."

Lily's eyes flashed with anger, her fingers curling into fists in her lap. "This isn't about him, Jet. This is about you not trusting *me*. Do you even hear yourself right now? You're acting like I'm some child who doesn't know what she's doing!"

Jet clenched the wheel as he struggled to keep his temper in check. "Maybe I'm just trying to protect you, Lily. You're seventeen—"

"And you're twenty-three!" Lily cut him off, her voice trembling with emotion. "I get it, Jet, you're older, wiser, whatever. But that doesn't give you the right to treat me like I'm incapable of making my own decisions."

The tension in the car was palpable, both of them breathing heavily, filling the space between them. Jet looked away, his voice muted but strained. "I just don't want to see you get taken advantage of."

Lily softened at his words, her anger ebbing away as she reached for his hand, her fingers brushing against his. "Jet, you have to trust me. If we're gonna work, you have to trust that I know what I'm doing."

"It's not you I don't trust, Lily. I thought you knew that!"

"Jet, you have to let me grow up! You're not going to be around for every situation. I mean, what are you going to do when you're on tour?"

"Well, that's simple ... you're quitting. I've already talked to Wallace and he agrees. You need to be studying for your GCSEs."

Lily's anger flared again, her face flushing with heat. "You what?! Now you're dictating my work schedule and conspiring with my grandfather!? Jesus, I am not a child!" She slammed back against the seat, folding her arms across her chest, the leather squeaking beneath her.

"As long as you keep acting like one, you'll be treated like one!" Jet snapped, his voice biting.

Frustrated, her anger boiling over now, she reached for the door handle, the cold metal stinging against her palm. As it opened, Jet called out, his voice rough with warning. "Don't you do it! Do not get out of this car!"

She glared at him, her eyes blazing with defiance, and in one swift movement, she stepped out, slamming the door shut behind her with a sharp crack that echoed through the car park. Jet watched as she stormed away, her figure growing smaller with each step. *God dammit, girl.* He blew out a heavy sigh; the realization hitting him like a punch to the gut. *Ugh ... Girl? Shit ... is she right? Am I treating her like a child? Fuck! Fuck! ... Fuuck!* Jet got out of the car and jogged after her. "Hey, Lil, wait up."

She continued walking, her shoulders tense, ignoring him. "Lily, please ... I'm sorry."

She stopped, her back still turned to him. He caught up to her, his hand gently resting on her shoulder, his touch hesitant. She turned slowly; her face streaked with tears, her lips trembling. Grabbing her, he pulled her close, both arms wrapping around her tightly as if afraid to let go. She let out a soft sob into his chest, her body shaking against his. "I don't like fighting with you." Her voice muffled, her arms finally wrapping around him in return. "It makes my heart hurt."

"Me too, Lil, me too." They stood there, holding each other as the world around them faded away, the sounds of the town growing distant, leaving only the steady rhythm of their breathing.

Eventually, Lily pulled back, her eyes red but calm, her fingers still gripping his shirt. "Let's get you home," Jet said softly, his voice laced with guilt. Even though nothing had been resolved, they both knew the conversation was over for now. They needed a break—a chance to cool off.

Friday evening, same place, same time. The sun seemed to hang lower in the sky this day. Jet sat in his car outside Lily's workplace, his mind still racing with thoughts of yesterday's argument. He knew they hadn't resolved anything yet, but tonight, they had the entire night to talk. Lily was supposed to be spending the night with Penny's sister Catherine—a cover story they'd tell her family so they could have time alone together. Deciding to put their issue aside for the ride home, Jet resolved to talk things through properly tonight.

Jet stepped inside the cafe, the scent of fresh coffee and pastries filling the air. The familiar chime of the bell above the door rang out, and he scanned the room, searching for Lily. His heart stopped when he saw her in the back corner, laughing with the same guy they had argued about the day before. The guy leaned in closer to her, his hand brushing against hers. Jet's blood boiled as he noticed the guy's smug grin, the way his fingers lingered on hers a second too long.

Jet's fists clenched involuntarily, his nails digging into his palms as he watched the scene unfold. His vision narrowed, his heart pounding in his chest. Just as he was about to call out to her, the guy made a move—leaning in to kiss her. Lily immediately backed away, clearly uncomfortable, but Jet's rage surged. Blindly, he stormed across the cafe, the sound of his boots heavy on the tiled floor.

"Get your hands off her!" Jet's voice was low but filled with fury, the words cutting through the cafe's noise like a knife.

The guy barely had time to react before Jet's fist connected with his jaw, sending him stumbling backward, his back colliding with a nearby table. The cafe fell silent as chairs scraped against the floor, and customers turned to watch the confrontation, their murmurs growing louder.

The guy recovered quickly, his eyes flashing with anger as he swung back at Jet, his fist slamming into Jet's ribs. Pain shot through Jet's side, but he barely registered it as they grappled, knocking over tables and chairs in their scuffle. Lily's voice rang out, shouting for them to stop, but the fight had already spiraled out of control.

Lily screamed again, her voice breaking through the chaos as she tried to push her way between them, desperate to break it up. "Jet, stop it! Please!"

In the frenzy, one of them shoved the other too hard, and their momentum sent them crashing into Lily. She lost her balance, her feet slipping on the tiled floor as she fell hard against the edge of a table before crumpling to the ground. Pain shot through her side, sharp and overwhelming, and she gasped, her vision blurring from the shock. The cold floor pressed against her cheek as she lay there, struggling to catch her breath.

"Lily!" Jet's voice broke through the haze, filled with panic as he rushed to her side. The cafe manager stood back, his face pale, unsure of what to do, while the other employees and customers watched in stunned silence.

Jet knelt beside Lily, his hands trembling as he gently lifted her into a sitting position, his heart pounding in his ears. "Lil, I'm so sorry. Are you okay? Talk to me."

Lily winced, her hand clutching her side where she'd hit the table. Tears filled her eyes, a mix of pain and frustration. Her voice was strained, barely above a whisper. "I'm fine, Jet. Just—why? Why did you have to do this?"

Her words cut through Jet's anger, leaving only regret in their wake. He looked at her, truly seeing the hurt in her eyes, and realized how badly he'd messed up. The cafe felt stifling now, the once comforting smell of coffee now nauseating.

"I'm sorry, Lil," he whispered, his voice thick with emotion. "I—I couldn't stand the thought of him touching you, and I didn't think. I just reacted."

Lily shook her head, her tears blurring her vision as she wiped them away with the back of her hand. "I told you, Jet. I love you. But if you keep doing this—keep letting your jealousy or whatever this is control you—"

The weight of her words sank into Jet's chest like a heavy stone, and for the first time, he fully grasped the consequences of his actions. He reached out, gently brushing a strand of hair from her face, his touch feather-light. "I don't want to lose you, Lil. I'm sorry."

The cafe manager approached cautiously, his expression a mix of concern and frustration as he glanced between them. "Is everything okay here? Do we need to call someone?"

Lily shook her head, her voice soft but firm. "No, it's okay. We're leaving."

With Jet's help, she got to her feet, wincing at the sharp pain in her side as she stood. Jet wrapped his arm around her, supporting her as they made their way out of the cafe. The cool evening air hit them as they stepped outside, a stark contrast to the suffocating atmosphere inside.

As they reached the car, the cafe manager called after them, his voice carrying a hint of guilt and resentment. "By the way, Daria, you're fired."

Lily turned to face him, her voice steady but filled with anger. "No, I quit!" She looked up at Jet, her eyes still glistening with tears but a hint of determination shining through. Jet stopped, turning to face Lily fully, his expression softening.

"I'm sorry, Lil. I know I keep saying it, but I really mean it. I'll do whatever it takes to fix this, to fix us."

Lily looked up at him, her tears finally drying, but the pain was still apparent. Despite everything, she could see the sincerity, the remorse, and the love that fueled his mistakes. She sighed softly, her voice barely above a whisper. "I'm sorry, too. I should've listened to you. You were right. That guy was a jerk, and I didn't see it because he was my boss. But you've got to let me learn the lessons, Jet. I was getting ready to punch him myself." She let out a small laugh, only to wince in pain, clutching her side.

Jet half-laughed, relief washing over him. "I would've liked to have seen that."

"Next time, let me!"

"Well, let's hope there isn't a next time."

As they got into the car, the sun dipped below the horizon, casting a warm orange glow across the town. The tension between them eased, but they both knew they had more to work through. Still, for now, they were together, and that was enough.

The drive home was quiet, but the silence between them felt less oppressive now. Jet glanced over at Lily every so often, his gaze filled with concern and guilt. She noticed but said nothing, her mind still processing everything that had happened. When they finally pulled up to his garage flat, Jet hurried to help her out of the car, his hand gently guiding her as they made their way inside.

As soon as the door closed behind them, the familiar comfort of his home settled around them, the tension of the outside world slipping away. Lily sighed deeply, leaning against the wall as she kicked off her shoes, wincing at the lingering pain in her side. Jet hovered nearby, his eyes searching hers for any sign of lingering anger.

"Lil…" he began, but she cut him off with a soft smile, shaking her head.

"Jet, it's okay. We've both said enough for today."

She stepped closer to him, her eyes softening as she looked up at him, the weight of the earlier battle already fading. His breath caught as he noticed the glint in her eyes, the way her lips parted slightly, inviting him in. He reached out, his hand brushing her cheek, his thumb tracing along the curve of her jaw. The warmth of his touch sent a familiar shiver down her spine, and she tilted her head into his palm, closing her eyes for a moment.

"I love you, Lil," Jet whispered, his voice husky with emotion.

"I love you too," she replied, her voice soft and forgiving. "Now, shut up and kiss me."

Jet didn't need to be told twice. He closed the distance between them, his lips crashing into hers with a hunger that had been building since their argument yesterday. The kiss was fierce, a mix of apology and desire, their bodies pressing together as if trying to erase the space that had grown between them.

Lily's fingers tangled in Jet's hair, pulling him closer as she deepened the kiss, her lips moving against his with a desperate need. His hands slid down her back, pulling her flush against him, careful to avoid the spot where she'd been hurt. Their breath mingled, hot and heavy, as the kiss grew more intense, both of them pouring everything they had into it.

When they finally pulled apart, gasping for air, their foreheads rested against each other's, their breaths mingling in the small space between them. Jet's eyes searched hers, finding only love and forgiveness there.

"We'll figure this out, Jet," Lily murmured, her fingers tracing the edge of his jaw. "Together."

He nodded, his voice rough with emotion. "Together."

They stood there, wrapped in each other's arms. The kiss may have only been a bandage over a deeper wound, but for now, it was enough to remind them of what they had and what they were willing to fight for.

Chapter Twenty

Let's Get Real

(2013)

"MAMA!" she heard Jack scream. She stepped out of the house. *Where is he?* She listened for his cries again. "MAMA! AHHH STOP!" Her heart leaped into her throat. *The barn!* Without a second thought, she started running. Bursting through the barn door, her worst fears materialized before her eyes: Levi had his hands on Jack, lifting and shaking him.

She slowed to grab the first thing she could use as a weapon. Gripping the handle of the shovel tightly, she wasted no time in swinging it with all her might. The flat back of the blade made contact between his shoulders. He dropped Jack, turning toward her, stumbling and glaring in disbelief.

"I told you, God dammit!" She swung again, hitting him in the side with the blade's edge, slicing through his shirt and into the flesh of his waist; she saw blood.

He went down.

"Jack, get in the house, now!" He got up and ran.

Stepping slowly and deliberately over to where Levi was kneeling, still gripping the shovel. "I told you I would kill you if you ever touched him again!" She circled him as he struggled to regain his bearings.

Holding his side where the blade had sliced through him, he lifted his hand to see the blood. "Fuck you! When I get up, you're dead, bitch!"

That was the breaking point. Jack was now ten, and after years of enduring Levi's abuse, turmoil, and violent temper, Daria had finally reached her limit. This was the last straw. An instinctive need to protect her son surged from deep within her, taking over completely. She moved on autopilot, her training guiding her without conscious thought, instinctively knowing exactly where to strike for maximum effectiveness.

She circled even closer and swung as he tried to stand. *Solar Plexus.* Then, again. *Achilles.* And again. *Throat.* And again. *Spine.* Every time he recoiled, it meant he could get up and take revenge. Every moan meant another threat. And that meant she could never let him get up again. She continued hitting and slicing him, calculating every swing of the shovel.

When he stopped moving, she ended her attack, stared at his limp and bloodied body, and waited for signs of life. When she was satisfied that he would not get up and retaliate, she dropped the shovel and stood over him.

She debated on whether to just bury him where he lay or call for help. She decided she needed to check on Jack.

"Jack! Where are you, baby?" she yelled as she slammed through the front door. She found him hiding in their bedroom between the wall and the bed where the nightstand sat.

She ran to him, checking him from head to toe. "Are you okay? Did he hurt you?" He pointed to his arms.

Daria recalled Levi shaking Jack by his upper arms. She carefully removed Jack's shirt and discovered Levi's handprints were still visible on Jack's skin, appearing red and painful. She immediately picked up Jack and headed towards the kitchen, where the house phone hung on the wall. Wasting no time, she dialed the number written next to the phone.

Jack was crying, not so much from the pain but from the panic of the situation. Uncle answered. "I need you; bring the doctor," is all she said, then hung up and tried to settle Jack. They were there within a half hour.

When she heard the car pull up, she carefully laid Jack, who had fallen asleep in her arms, on the couch. She opened the door, finding Uncle and the doctor walking towards the house. Without waiting for them, she walked past them and headed straight to the barn. Uncle quickly turned and followed.

The two stood at the entrance, staring at Levi's limp and bloodied body. Finally, Uncle spoke. "I wondered how long it would take."

Daria, unphased by Uncle's sarcasm, stood stone-faced as the doctor walked up behind them, glanced around Uncle, and snorted a 'humph' at her distaste for the situation.

"Is he dead?" Uncle asked.

"I hope so."

The doctor gave Daria a sly half-grin as the two women turned to head for the house. She wasn't sure if it was a smile of approval, but that's how she was going to take it.

Daria yelled back to him. "He's your problem now."

She stood at the front door watching as Uncle dragged the body to the trunk of his car and plopped it in. They both heard an audible groan as he closed the trunk lid.

"So ... not dead." Uncle wiped his hands with his handkerchief and put it back in his pocket on the way to his driver's side door.

"If he comes back here, he will be," yelling matter-of-factly. She turned and walked into the house, where the doctor was checking on Jack.

The doctor smiled at Jack and ruffled his hair as she stood and finished her observation. She informed Daria, "He will likely bruise but I see no other injuries." Turning her attention back to Jack, she smiled. " I believe Uncle has some sweets in his pocket." Jack made a beeline out the door to find Uncle. "What are your plans?" Daria watched as Uncle dug out a handful of hard candies and placed a few in Jack's hand. She asked again, "Will you stay here in your home, or will you leave now that Levi will not be returning?"

Daria paused, turned back to the doctor, and contemplated. *So, she's sure Levi definitely won't be back?* She tried to rationalize that fact, knowing it had to come to fruition. If Levi survived his wounds and returned, she and Jack would never be safe. He would most assuredly retaliate.

She came to the conclusion that they *all* understood that Levi would have to die of his wounds, or Uncle would have to finish what she started. Either way was fine with her at this point. Damn the consequences.

But would there be any consequences? Over the last decade, Levi had made more enemies than friends. Would anyone even bother searching for him? Would anyone even care? The answers to all her inner questions were clear, and she assumed that Uncle would have to handle anything else that arose, so she put it out of her mind and answered the doctor.

"Jack's home is here, with his friends and school," she said, looking back out the window and watching as Jack ran around Uncle, tugging at his pockets in search of more candy. "Besides, we have a farm to run."

"So, you won't go back to England?"

"To what? That dream died the day I arrived here. You've made sure of that. Besides, I'm sure that ship has sailed," she pointed out, almost to herself, a bitter edge in her tone. "All I have left of him is his son, and that'll have to be enough." At least, that's what she told herself in order to get through her days.

The doctor, approving of Daria's state of mind, nodded and left.

As Daria looked out the front window and watched the doctor and Uncle say their goodbyes to Jack. She couldn't help but reflect on a time when she thought those dreams were just beginning.

Chapter Twenty-One

First Love

(2001)

It was the end of July. Lily was seventeen, soon to be eighteen in a couple of weeks. Her classes had finished, and Jet flew her to the States to finish the rest of the tour with them.

It was her first time seeing them in an actual concert arena. All the shows she had been to up until then were small venues and halls, but since the band had finally agreed on a management team, they were soaring into the mainstream music world.

The open-air concert arena was a sprawling, pulsating entity, alive with the energy of thousands of fans eagerly waiting for the show to start. Towering speakers and elaborate light rigs adorned the massive stage while beams of light cut through the darkness, sweeping across the audience in a kaleidoscope of colors. Lily stood in the entrance hall where the band would appear from on their cart, ready to get to the stage. Her heart raced as she took it all in, the anticipation building with every passing moment.

The backstage area was a hive of activity. Vick, the FOH sound engineer, hurried about, checking equipment, adjusting sound levels, and coordinating the complex choreography that kept the show running smoothly. JD, Jets guitar tech, passed by, giving her a thumbs-up, recognizing her as Jet's girlfriend. She nodded back, a small smile playing on her lips. Everyone could feel the buzz of anticipation as the crew made final preparations for the curtain to rise.

This is insane. Lily thought. *I've never seen anything like this. This is it; they've made it, they've really made it.* Feeling a mix of pride and nerves.

This was a whole new level of performance. They were opening for one of the legends of rock, and she was right in the middle of it. She felt a hand on her shoulder as she stood there, taking it all in. Lily turned to see Jet. His face lit up with excitement.

"Hey, you ready for this?" Grinning from ear to ear.

"More than ready. Oh my God, Jet. This is amazing." She was absolutely giddy for him.

"And it's only going to get bigger from here, Lil. Come on, I wanna show you something."

He led her through the maze of equipment and people, guiding her to the side of the stage. From there, she had a perfect view of the audience, a vast expanse of people stretching out into the darkness, all waiting for the show to start.

He stood next to her, one arm over her shoulder, pointing from off stage. "Look at that, Lil. All these people, they're here for us. Well ... they will be—one day."

"Of course, they're here for you. Why else would they come early if they were only here for the headliner?"

"Yeah, well, it's just the beginning. One of these days *we're* gonna be the headliner. We've got so much more to do."

"You're already my headliner!"

Jet blushed a little as he leaned in for a kiss. "You've always been my biggest fan."

"Damn straight!" She crossed her arms, looking out at the audience.

The lights dimmed, and the crowd roared in anticipation. "I gotta go, babe." Jet gave her a quick kiss on the cheek before running out onto the stage, greeted by an explosion of cheers. Ronny patted her head as he passed and Reggie was right behind him, hand up, waiting for a high five as he ran by. The band launched into their first song, and the energy in the arena rocketed.

Lily watched from the wings, her heart swelling with pride for the boys. Jet was in his element, his charisma and talent captivating the audience. She could see the love and admiration in the faces of the fans, mirroring her own.

This is where they belong. This is definitely where Jet is meant to be.

As the concert progressed, Lily swayed to the rhythm, singing the lyrics to every song. She danced with abandon. Each note resonated deeply within her, and her eyes never left Jet. She watched him command the stage, his presence magnetic. She felt a bond tighten between them, a silent exchange of triumph and joy.

During a break between songs, Jet glanced over at her, giving her a wink and a smile. That smile said everything—gratitude, love, and the promise of many more nights like this.

When their set finally ended, the applause was deafening. Jet and the band took their bows, basking in the crowd's adoration. Backstage, the atmosphere was electric with celebration. Jet came to her, his face glowing with happiness.

"So, what did you think?"

"It was incredible. You were incredible. Everything was incredible!" She beamed.

"That's because I had my best girl with me," Jet laughed.

He pulled her into a hug, and for a moment, they were the only two people in the arena. In that embrace, Lily felt that all was right with the world. She was where she was supposed to be, and so was he. All of their shared dreams were on their way to coming true.

About that time, the tour manager tapped Jet on the shoulder. "You got another one in ya?" He thumbed behind him to the audience.

The crowd still roaring for more, Jet pulled back slightly, a mischievous glint in his eye. He looked over at the boys still toweling off and nodded for them to follow. "Yeah, we got one more."

Reggie was like, "Dude, we've played everything."

"We're gonna do the new one."

Ronny and Reggie looked at Jet in recognition.

"You sure?" Ronny glanced at Lily with a half smile, knowing what was coming.

"Yeah, I'm sure," Jet said.

Jet turned back to the stage and grabbed the microphone as he and the rest of the band followed. "How's everyone doing tonight?" The crowd roared. "I guess we're not done here!" He waited a moment for the crowd to settle. "But before we go, I've got someone special I want you all to meet."

The crowd quieted, a wave of curiosity rippling through them.

"Hey Lily, why don't you come on out," he said, holding out his hand to her.

Lily's eyes widened in shock. She hadn't expected this. The crowd turns, some craning their necks to catch a glimpse of her.

"Don't be shy, Lily. Come on."

Cameras turned toward her, Lily's face now on the screens behind the band. The crowd's cheers grew louder as she put her hands up, waving him off and shaking her head. Now, the roar was a mix of laughter and encouragement. Chanting, "Lil-y! Lil-y! Lil-y!"

She hesitated, but the warmth in his eyes gave her courage. Lily walked out, her hands over her face, hiding her embarrassment. Jet met her halfway. She took his hand and let him lead her onto the stage. The crowd erupted in applause and cheers as Jet wrapped an arm around her shoulders.

"This is Lily," he announced to the audience. "She's my inspiration and my muse, and I wanted to share this moment with her."

The audience's reaction was overwhelming, their applause and cheers echoing in the massive arena. Lily felt a rush of emotion, tears welling up in her eyes. She looked up at Jet and he smiled down at her, his love shining through. He pulled his guitar strap over his shoulder and strummed the chords. "This ones for you, Lil."

JD brought a stool out from offstage for her to sit on as a dreamy rock ballad slowly began building. Jet sang the words to the audience, but as he reached the chorus, he turned to her, gazing deeply into her eyes.

In your arms, I've found my place,
With every heartbeat, I see your face,
It's the first time I've known this feeling so true,
I've fallen, I've fallen in love with you.

The crowd melted away as Lily gazed back into Jet's eyes and the world disappeared as the song ended.

As the applause continued, Jet leaned down and kissed her softly on the lips. The crowd went wild, and Lily felt like she was floating, the reality of the moment sinking in.

This is it. This is our real beginning.

Chapter Twenty-Two

Rene

(2016)

As time went by, Daria took on the responsibility of running the farm with the help of a few hired hands. She worked tirelessly day in and day out, tending to the crops, feeding the livestock, and managing the finances.

Jack, now a teenager, had grown into a determined, hardworking young man, eager to take on more responsibilities. He loved the farm and dreamed of turning it into a productive dairy business. Daria often watched him with pride, wishing she could share it with Jet. But she knew Jet would have been just as proud of the young man their son was becoming.

Daria had always been uneasy about the bond between Uncle and Jack, but being the pragmatic mother she was, she understood the importance of having a strong male figure in Jack's life. Levi had not been that. Like it or not, Uncle fit the bill, and she truly believed that he genuinely cared for her son.

Despite the strained beginnings of their relationship, Uncle had taken Jack under his wing, also teaching him skills and taking him on adventures. But there was always a shadow hanging over their time together, a reminder of the control Uncle still held over their lives.

Now at thirteen, Jack's interests had grown beyond farm life. Jack's attention was drawn to new things, including a girl he met at the Kentucky Junior Livestock Expo.

The FFA fair was buzzing with energy. Booths displaying everything from livestock to agricultural innovations lined the extensive field. Jack, in his eighth-grade year, wandered through the maze of displays, taking in the sights and sounds. He stopped at a booth showcasing different breeds of cattle, admiring the sleek, well-groomed animals.

"Pretty cool, huh?" a voice said beside him.

Jack turned to see a girl his age, her auburn hair tied back in a neat ponytail, wearing an FFA jacket. Her bright green eyes sparkled with enthusiasm.

"Yeah, they are," Jack replied, smiling.

The girl's attention was still on the display, but Jack stood there, unable to take his eyes off her. Finally, he managed, "Uh, hi, I'm Jack."

"Renee," she said, turning and extending her hand.

They shook hands, and Jack couldn't help but feel an immediate kinship with Renee. It was obvious to him that they must share a passion for farming and animals.

As Renee turned to walk away, Jack wasn't ready to let her leave his company. He pointed to a bull on the display and asked, "Hey, Renee … any idea what breed this one is?" He knew full well what breed it was.

She stepped back up to the booth. "Oh, he's a beaut! That's a Brahma."

"Yeah, that's right. Now I remember. Hey, where are you headed next?"

"Rabbits."

"Mind if I hang with you for a while? This is my first time here."

Renee smiled and tucked a loose strand of hair behind her ear, answering a little too quickly, "No, not at all."

They walked together, talking. Jack learned that Renee's family owned a dairy farm close to his home, though in the next county.

"Have you seen the livestock judging competition?" Renee asked. "It's starting soon. My family has a heifer entered."

"Really? I'd love to see that."

They made their way to the judging area, where a crowd had already gathered. Jack watched as Renee's heifer was paraded before the judges. The pride in her eyes was unmistakable.

"She's beautiful."

"Thanks," Renee replied, beaming. "We've worked hard to get her ready for this."

As the competition continued, Jack found himself more and more impressed by Renee's knowledge and passion for farming. They cheered together when her heifer won first place, and Jack couldn't help but feel a surge of excitement for her.

After the competition, they wandered back to the main area of the fair, sharing stories about their experiences on the farm, laughing at each other's jokes, and discovering they had a lot in common.

"Do you want to grab some ice cream?" Jack suggested, pointing to a nearby stand.

"Sure," Renee said. "But, my treat, since my heifer won."

They sat on a bench, enjoying their ice cream and the warm afternoon sun. Jack felt a warmth in his chest that had nothing to do with the weather. He knew he had met someone special, someone who understood him in a way few others at school did.

As the day drew to a close, they exchanged phone numbers and promised to keep in touch. Jack watched as Renee walked away, her presence lingering in his thoughts. Just then, one of Uncle's men walked up behind him and put a hand on Jack's shoulder.

"Am I going to get to see her again?" Jack asked, still watching her disappear into the crowd.

"That's up to your Uncle. Time to get home."

Chapter Twenty-Three

Decisions

(2021)

When Uncle took Jack for the first time, Daria resigned herself to the reality that she was trapped. Every attempt at escape had been thwarted or discovered. At this point, she figured the odds of breaking free from this life were slim, and Jack needed to come first. Like it or not, the doctor was right—he needed stability and a nurturing environment.

After Levi's demise, things actually improved. Sort of. Though her movements were still closely monitored, her agreement to train with Uncle allowed her time away from the farm. With her good behavior and assistance in local operations, they were granted a landline for local calls, primarily for emergencies or when Uncle needed to reach her.

However, over the past few years, Uncle's visits had become less frequent, and last year, the trips stopped altogether. Uncle was at least in his mid-fifties when he grabbed Daria, and now his health was failing. She often wondered what would happen to them if he died.

Jack and Renee, though living in neighboring counties, attended the same high school, where Jack eventually asked her to be his girlfriend. Despite many attempts by Uncle to keep them apart, their connection grew stronger and there was very little Uncle could do about it, eventually giving into Jack's demands for more freedoms.

In school, Jack and Rene took agriculture classes that taught livestock production, and in the evening, Jack enrolled in online courses at the local library and became friendly with other local dairy farmers who helped him join the local co-op, which taught him the business side.

Then, on Jack's eighteenth birthday, a package arrived. Daria thought it might be a present for Jack from Uncle or maybe his family. There was no postmark, so she had no idea where it came from. She ripped open the top corner and peeked inside. It was a gift.

She set the package on the table next to the door and waited for Jack to get home so they could open it together. She made his favorite meal, steak and fries, and baked him a chocolate cake.

After dinner, she gave him her present. "Oh, I almost forgot!" She ran, grabbed the package, and handed it to him. "This came today."

"What is it?"

"I assume it's for you. I peeked, and it was wrapped in gift wrap, so, maybe it's from Uncle or his family. Open it." She was happy that someone had remembered him.

He opened it to find a large leather portfolio tied closed with a leather string. "Huh, that's a weird present. It's old, and it's already full of papers."

"Here, let me have it," his mother said, holding her hand out.

"Why would someone send me that?

She unwound the leather string and pulled out the papers. On top was the deed to the property, along with deeds to the adjacent properties surrounding the farm. She pulled those off and set them on the table. Jack picked them up to look at them. "Is this what I think it is?"

The next set of papers made Daria's knees go weak. She pulled a chair out and plopped down. Curiosity sparked in Jack's eyes as he examined her dazed expression. He walked over and took the top paper from her hand.

"This can't be right; the names are all wrong. He's my—" He looked back at his mother, who sat paralyzed. Daria gazed into Jack's concerned eyes, struggling to find the right words to explain. "Mom, what is this?" Jack's eyes widened with a mixture of confusion and worry. Then he knelt before her. "Mom, what is it? Talk to me."

She took a deep breath and gently cupped his face. "The names are right; Levi was not your father."

He stood up, took the rest of the papers from her, and looked through them. Along with his genuine birth certificate with his biological father's name on it, he found a passport for each of them, all of her original identification, and a bank book with a balance of a little over seven hundred and fifty thousand dollars.

He sat in the chair in front of her, silently going through the papers over and over, trying to make sense of them all. "Mom, you gotta talk to me."

She got up from her seat, walked over to the kitchen cabinet, grabbed two glasses and a half-empty bottle of bourbon, then poured a two-finger serving for both of them. She shot hers down and poured another. After she downed that one, she pointed to his glass; Jack shook his head, and when she saw he was not interested in drinking, she downed his glass, too.

With her head tilted back, holding the glass close to her mouth, she accepted every last drop. Loudly slapping the glass down on the table, she closed her eyes, allowing the smooth amber liquid a moment to take effect. She sat quietly as the warm numbness seeped through her body before taking a deep breath. "Jack, I need you to know that I love you with every ounce of my being."

"I know that, mom."

Daria looked into Jack's eyes, her heart heavy with the weight of the truth she was about to reveal. "Also, I am desperately sorry for everything I am about to tell you. And I hope you will understand why I haven't said anything till now."

Jack's expression shifted from confusion to concern. "What do you mean, Mom?" She went on to share the condensed version of her life and the love his father had finally found for her.

"I thought I might be pregnant, so after a band meeting one day, I asked to borrow his car so I could go to the drugstore. He drove me instead. When we got there, he stayed outside to talk to the schoolmate he ran into while I went in to get a pregnancy test, and that's when Uncle grabbed me, drugged me, and I woke up here. I never had the chance to tell him about you. He didn't know that's why we were there. I didn't want to say anything until I knew for sure, and that's the part that kills me every day. He's missed everything from your birth to now."

"So, why didn't you go to him after Dad—I mean, Levi disappeared?"

"Hun, I'm sure he had long since moved on, and at that point, you came first. This is the only home you've ever known, and you love this place.

"You know, my whole life, everything I ever loved was taken from me. In my childhood, I lost my mother, along with my trust and my innocence. Despite it being for the best, I still had to let her go. As a teen, I lost my grandmother, and when I became an adult, my heart and soul were ripped away." She reached over and rubbed his cheek with her knuckles, then smiled. "I got some of that back when you came along. You have his crooked smile." Locking eyes with him, she added, "I wasn't going to let that happen to you, too."

Jack sat at the table with his mom, considering everything she said. "This is insane; I can't even begin to wrap my head around what you've been through ... Why didn't you ever say anything?"

"Who was I going to tell? You were a child, Jack. Was I supposed to burden you with all this? Besides you and Uncle are so close, was I suppose to take that from you. Or trust that you wouldn't let a plan to escape get back to him? I couldn't take the chance that he would retaliate or restrict us even further. You know how protective he is of you. Whether I like it or not he was good to you. Good *for* you." Tears pricked her eyes. "And this ..." She leaned in, pointing to the papers. "Is a good thing, Jack ... no, it's a great thing." she corrected herself. "It's proof that he loves you. Do you understand? Besides, this is every parent's dream, Jack. To be able to watch their child's dream come true. Do you know how far ahead of the game you are with free land and the money to make something out of it?"

"Mom, I think you should take the money."

"Absolutely not."

"Why?"

"I won't have any part of it."

"But—"

"Jack, it came from a source that almost destroyed me. Taking it would only lend legitimacy to the shit I've endured. Like I was being paid off or something, and there's not enough money in the world that could do that. Besides, it belongs to you; you'll never know what all they took from you, what can't be replaced. If anyone deserves it, it's you; do something good with it. Use it to build your dream."

He stared at the papers, still absorbing the gravity of everything he had heard that night. Finally, looking up into his mother's eyes, he started to say something, but she interrupted him. "I'm sorry, Hun, but this place doesn't mean to me what it means to you. It's never been my home. And if I'm being honest, I'm glad to be free of it. This is your home now. I want you to love it, nurture it, and raise me a bunch of grandbabies that I can visit."

"Are you leaving?"

"No, of course not. I wouldn't just leave you. I want to make sure you're settled. There's a lot to do now that we have a plan for this place. Right?"

He nodded and smiled, relieved that he wasn't losing his mother right away. "But when you do ... where would you go?"

She half laughed. " Honestly, I hadn't thought that far out yet. I'm not sure."

"Do you want to go find him?"

"It's not that simple, Hun. I wouldn't even know where to begin to look for him. He and his band could be anywhere."

He thought for a moment. "You could start in his hometown." Hinting at what he wanted to say earlier.

"I suppose that would be a good starting point. His family may still be there." Her chest welled up with all those old feelings and she needed to end this line of questions. "I don't know. It's a moot point. I'm not going anywhere, anytime soon, so let's shelve this conversation for another time." She patted his hand and said, "I need some more of that cake."

Over the course of the next six months, they fenced off the new properties. Cattle were now grazing, and they had constructed the new milking barn. Jack and his high-school sweetheart, Renee, were just a week away from their nuptials.

Daria was sitting at the kitchen table, going over the last of the farm books and vendors with Renee. "You gotta keep your eye on Paul Duggar's team. They do good work, but they can get lazy if you're not right there watching them." The phone rang, and Daria got up to answer it. "Hello? ... oh, I see ... I'm sorry to hear that. Yes, of course. Thank you. Take care."

Jack walked in, the screen door screeching closed. "Who was that?"

Daria stood silent for a moment after hanging up, not quite sure how to process the news she had just received. "That was the doctor," she said. "Uncle passed."

"What? I knew he was ill, but I thought we had more time?"

"She said it happened quickly; she was just as surprised. No funeral, just a cremation, and then they'll take his ashes home to his family."

Jack, clearly overcome by the news, walked over to his mother and embraced her. Tears streamed down her cheeks as a sense of relief washed over her, followed by a wave of guilt for even allowing herself to feel that way.

For almost two decades, Uncle and the doctor had been a constant source of suffering for her, but despite her situation, they had been a blessing for Jack and, through him, somewhat of a blessing for her. Confused by her feelings, more tears fell as she held her son even tighter, acutely aware of the significant loss he must be feeling right now.

When Jack regained his composure, he pulled away from his mother, giving her a reassuring smile. He walked over to the desk, hesitated a moment, then opened the drawer and pulled something out.

"Mom, I was going to give this to you after the wedding, but I think now's as good a time as any."

Confused, she watched as Jack handed her an envelope. She opened it and pulled out the contents. It contained a credit card in her name and an airline ticket.

"What's this?"

"Mom, I'm settled. Renee and I can run this place now, and you need to start your life or at least get some of it back."

"Hun, I can't accept this."

Renee glanced at Jack, cautious not to overstep. He responded with a half-nodding smile of approval. Encouraged, she gently reached for Daria's hand. "Jack ... told me how you came to be here and that you didn't want any of the original money. We've learned so much from you over these last months, and we wanted to pay you back in some way. So, we've established an account for you, drawing only from the farm's profits. I must say, with your head for business and without mortgages and building loans, our only bills are overhead. We've been fortunate, and we want to share that with you. You deserve it. You've probably worked harder than any of us to build this place into what it is now. We've talked about it—a lot—and we want you to know that we can take it from here."

"But this is too much. I can't—"

"Spend the money, don't spend the money, but at least use the ticket," Jack said.

Daria stared at the ticket. "It's one way. Are you trying to get rid of me?" She smiled through her tears.

"I don't expect you'll be needing a round-trip ticket, but if you do, you have the card. Rene and I would like nothing more than to go with you and get to the bottom of all this but it's calving season and we aren't even taking time for a honeymoon right now. Start in Leeds, go see his family and see if they can help." Daria nodded, accepting his advice. Jack walked over to his mother and held her by her shoulders. She looked up at him. "Mom, we've got this. So, now the question is," he said, pulling her in for a hug. "What's stopping you?"

She blew out a heavy sigh. "I guess nothing. That package ... was almost like an invitation, wasn't it?"

Rene pushed Daria's passport toward her on the table as Jack stepped away from Daria and sat next to Rene in a subtle sign of solidarity. "Go find him, mom. You have a right to be happy, too."

Viktor, Uncle's team leader, paced his small office atop the warehouse training facility, the weight of the recent news heavy on his shoulders. His contacts in the area reported that people were asking questions—risky questions. They were looking for Daria, and the inquiries were becoming more frequent. He had to act fast, but how? And should he tell Daria?

Unable to decide alone, Viktor grabbed his phone and dialed the doctor's number. She picked up after the second ring.

"Viktor, what is it?" Her voice was calm, but laced with concern.

"We've got a problem," Viktor began, his voice low. "I have reports of people asking around about Daria. My contacts say it's been happening for a few weeks now, and it's getting more difficult to shut them down."

There was a pause on the other end of the line before the doctor spoke. Her tone measured. "Do you know what they're after? Why now, after all this time?"

"No, not yet. But it doesn't feel right. They're being discreet, but word travels fast in certain circles. I'm afraid it won't be long before Daria or Jack catch wind of it."

She sighed, clearly weighing the situation. "Listen carefully, Viktor. I need you to dig deeper. Find out who's asking the questions, and what their intentions are. But under no circumstances are you to tell Daria or Jack. Not yet. We don't want to alarm them unless we know exactly what we're dealing with."

Viktor nodded, even though she couldn't see him. "Understood. I'll keep this quiet for now. But ... if this gets any worse—"

"I know, Viktor," the doctor interrupted gently. "As soon as you find anything concrete, let me know. We'll handle it from there. Just be careful. This could escalate quickly."

"I will," Viktor promised. "I'll be in touch as soon as I have something."

As he ended the call, Viktor knew he had to be cautious, but he also knew that whatever these people were up to, it was far from over. And Daria, whether she realized it or not, was at the center of it all.

To be continued ...